MAN CAMP

MAN CAMP

A Novel

ADRIENNE BRODEUR

RANDOM HOUSE NEW YORK

These are uncorrected proofs. Please do not quote for publication without checking your copy against the finished book.

This is a work of fiction. Names, characters, places, and incidents are the products of the author's imagination or are used fictitiously. Any resemblance to actual events, locales, or persons, living or dead, is entirely coincidental.

Published in the United States by Random House,
an imprint of The Random House Publishing Group,
a division of Random House, Inc., New York.

Random House and colophon are registered trademarks of Random House, Inc.

LIBRARY OF CONGRESS CATALOGING-IN-PUBLICATION DATA
Brodeur, Adrienne.
Man camp: a novel / Adrienne Brodeur.
p. cm.
ISBN 1-4000-6214-4
1. Self-actualization (Psychology)—Fiction. 2. Man-woman relationships—Fiction. 3. New York (N.Y.)—Fiction. 4. West Virginia—Fiction. 5. Family farms—Fiction. 6. Land tenure—Fiction. 7. Friendship—Fiction. 8. Farm life—Fiction. 9. Sex role—Fiction. 10. Camps—Fiction. I. Title.
PS3602.R6346M36 2005
813'.6—dc22 2004051470

Printed in the United States of America on acid-free paper

www.atrandom.com

246897531

First Edition

Book design by Lisa Sloane.

DEDICATION TK

ACKNOWLEDGMENTS TK

MAN CAMP

CHAPTER 1

> "The great question that I have not yet been able to answer, despite my thirty years of research into the feminine soul, is 'What does a woman want?' "
>
> *Sigmund Freud*

AS USUAL, Lucy Stone is waiting for Martha. She's worked late tonight and taken a cab straight from the labs to La Luna, the Chelsea wine bar where she now sits, wondering why she rushed. Martha is *never* on time. At least tonight, Lucy's come prepared with the current issue of *Biology Today,* which she has open to an article on the mating habits of swallows. The magazine lies on the stainless steel bar in front of her and Lucy holds a pen poised to take notes in the margin. Only she's not really reading, just trying to look occupied to avoid unwanted conversation. Her blonde hair is pulled back neatly and folded over in a large barrette, and she wears the thick, black-rimmed glasses of someone who wants to be taken seriously. But even at thirty-three, with a teaching position at Columbia University and the promise of a remarkable career, Lucy can't quite pull off the look of a seasoned biologist. When she tries, it has the opposite effect, making her seem young and even more approachable, the way a little girl never looks more like a little girl than when she's dressed up in her mother's high heels and party gown.

It's a quarter after nine, fifteen minutes past the time she and Martha agreed to meet, which means Martha still has five minutes before either of them considers her officially late. *Relax. She'll be here any minute,* Lucy tells herself, wondering what it would be like to be the type of self-confident woman who goes to nice bars by herself—just to read and have a glass of wine—and not worry what anyone around her thinks.

"Tonight's Martha's big night, right?" asks Eva, La Luna's plump bartender, as she pours Lucy a glass of red wine. "I can't believe she's going through with this half-baked plan." Eva only charges Lucy and Martha for one glass of wine no matter how much they drink. She says it's because they're good for business, but she has a crush on Martha and is well tipped by them in the process. More provocative than pretty, Eva is wearing her usual low-riding skirt, which reveals an ample swath of young belly and a tattoo—slightly parted lips—just below her navel.

Lucy nods. I can't believe it either, she thinks. But if anyone can pull it off, Martha can.

Lucy stares at the bowls of radishes placed along the bar and thinks of Scarlett O'Hara, retching in front of a burned-down Tara, wondering who actually likes radishes. But looking down the bar, she sees that everyone does. People are congregated around the bowls dunking radishes in sea salt and popping them into their mouths, which gives her a pang of homesickness for Cape Cod, where the typical bar fare is peanuts and Chex party mix. Here at La Luna, the food is complicated, full of flavors that take a certain will to tackle. Eva has explained to her that the food is meant to "challenge" the wine. *En garde,* Lucy thinks, and drops a radish into the salt, puts the whole thing into her mouth, and crunches down. Her eyes water slightly at the bitterness. She takes a sip of wine and has another radish. Then another.

"Hey there," says a handsome, sandy-haired man in his mid-thirties who has sidled up behind her.

Lucy turns on her stool and peers at him over her glasses.

"Hmm. Interesting," he says, reading the article's title over her shoulder: " 'The Mating Habits of Swallows.' " He lets out a low chuckle. "And from where I was sitting, you looked like such a nice girl."

Lucy smiles uncomfortably.

"Any good bird shots in there?" he says, laughing at his joke.

Lucy doesn't answer.

"I might not know a whole lot about swallows," he continues, "but some people consider me an *expert* on mating." He steps back with his hands on his hips so that his jacket spreads open.

Lucy recognizes the behavior as similar to that of the male ruffed grouse, a bird that makes itself look larger through chest-puffing and wing-stretching displays. She makes a mental note to include this behavior in the section of her research paper on male dominance. As Lucy looks the man over, she wonders if lines like the one he just used generally work for him and feels relieved that she no longer has to give a second thought to such advances since falling in love with Adam two years ago.

After a moment, the sandy-haired man becomes uneasy and lowers his arms so that his shoulders slump forward slightly. Then he shrugs and moves on.

Silence is a fairly new tactic for Lucy, one that Martha taught her. The old Lucy—single Lucy—would have laughed politely at his jokes even if she wasn't interested, only to spend the balance of the evening trying to shake him. Failing that, she might have agreed to a date with him if only to explain why she didn't want to date him, and it's conceivable there would have been a second encounter, a coffee, perhaps, to make sure that everything was resolved satisfactorily. Once, a few years back, when Lucy was trying to get rid of a persistent suitor, Martha—never a fan of her friend's accommodating approach—suggested that a blow job might be a nice way to let the guy down gently. That paved the way for Lucy's current, more direct communication policy.

Lucy goes back to pretending to read, but the bar is loud, crammed with hipsters from the art world—gorgeous twenty-somethings whose real talent lies in looking disheveled, with unwashed hair, scuffed shoes, and untucked shirttails. Lucy wills Martha to arrive.

To Martha's credit, she's been working hard on her time-management issues and not being late is one of her two New Year's resolutions. The second resolution, which was Lucy's idea, is for Martha to go out on at least one date a month. "Easy to say when you *have* a boyfriend," Martha chided her, but she knew it was a good idea and eventually agreed. Lucy's resolutions are to finish her postdoctoral fellowship paper, *Sexual Selection: What Humans Can Learn from Animals,* and to make sure that Martha goes out on that date every month. Martha only has ten days left to secure January's date, and it will be no small feat for Lucy to complete her research and write her paper in the next year. With this deadline in mind, Lucy underlines the first sentence of the article: "Female swallows invariably select for extreme tail feather length in males."

Martha arrives twenty minutes late on the dot. Snow is melting on her hair, and her curls have sprung into tight, dark spirals around her face. Pink-cheeked and positively glowing, she gives Lucy an enthusiastic hug that lifts her slightly off her stool. "Sorry I'm late," she says, smiling broadly. This is Martha's standard greeting and it rolls off her lips as easily as anyone else's "How are you?" or "Good to see you." Even her answering machine says, "Hi, This is Martha. Sorry I'm late. I'm on my way."

Lucy foregoes her usual lecturing look and pats the stool beside her. "Tell me everything."

Martha McKenna is an actress and she relishes attention. "Patience," she says, shrugging off her coat Gypsy Rose Lee–style, first the right shoulder, then the left, until it slides down her back. She's clad in the armor of the New York thirty-something single woman—designer everything (charged to maxed-out credit cards) and red, red lipstick. She's one of those women whose beauty lies in her imperfections, which are abundant and work in marvelous unison: her nose and chin are too pointy, her eyes slope downward and disappear into slits when she laughs, and she has a brilliant streak of white hair, which forms its own silvery twist, separate from the rest of her dark-brown curls. When she's not feeling old (she often describes herself as "close to forty" even though she just turned thirty-seven), she knows the streak is her sexiest feature.

Eva approaches with a bottle of Martha's favorite Chardonnay. "Hello, glamour-puss," she says, looking at Martha and batting her eyelashes flirtatiously. "Tonight's on me."

"Hi, sweetie," Martha says. "Regrettably, I'm still straight this week."

"You'll come around," Eva says, pouring Martha's wine. "So, how'd it go?" she asks, meaning how was the inaugural night of Martha's new business: FirstDate.

IT HAS BEEN THREE MONTHS since Martha came up with the concept for FirstDate, following a blind date with Simon Hodges, a man who thought the way to a woman's heart was through her ears. Even before their drinks arrived, Simon began reciting the lengthy and well-rehearsed story of his life: his hilarious childhood antics, his sober course of study at Harvard, his failed first marriage, his current success as a political historian. Throughout his speech, Martha contemplated how much scotch would be considered too much in polite company.

An eternity later, when they were on the sidewalk outside of the restaurant and the date's end was finally in sight, Martha scanned the horizon for on-duty lights, euphoric that the prospect of freedom was just one taxi ride away.

Simon cleared his throat. "I daresay, this has been a magical evening."

You daresay? Martha turned around and found herself looking directly into a pair of descending nostrils, dark and hairy, and moved quickly to avert a kiss on the mouth.

With his eyes still closed, Simon said, "If you're feeling even half the connection I am, just give me a sign. Any sign."

Martha considered her signage options. She could place her index finger to her temple and pull her thumb trigger, or wave an arm overhead, the universal signal for a swimmer in distress. Instead, she just got into a taxicab.

—

"How's it possible that a man Simon's age has no idea how to treat a woman on a first date?" Martha said to Lucy the following morning over steaming mugs of café au lait in Lucy's cluttered living room. Books and journals on the reproductive habits of various species overflowed from the bookshelves into neat stacks on the floor. "I didn't say three sentences the whole night, which Simon somehow managed to interpret as rapture. It might have been the worst first date of my entire life." Martha lit a cigarette. "What was yours again?"

"That's a toughie," Lucy said, sifting through her bad date memories. She'd had many like the one Martha described with Simon Hodges, dates where her role was to be impressed and seem interested. And she'd had the opposite, too. Dates where she was expected to do the impressing while the guy sat back and evaluated her performance.

"Seriously, last night represents an all-time dating low for me. Dull and opinionated is a deadly combo."

"Bad? Yes. An all-time dating low? No." Lucy had heard too many of Martha's dating stories over the years to fall for that one again. "You've gone out with more deserving contenders. Like that guy who sang opera to you over crème brûlée. Or what about the Boston blue blood you went out with? Lothrop?"

Martha imitated Lothrop's put-on Brahman accent: " 'I assume you've Googled me and know who I am.' "

"That's the one."

"I guess you're right. Lothrop trumps Simon," Martha agreed. "But let's not forget that I'm not the only one who has a history of bad dates, Miss Happily in Love."

"No argument here," Lucy said, recalling a first date who mentioned his wife so casually over their after-dinner drinks that she almost didn't register the remark. "In the five years we've known each other, we've dated momma's boys, narcissists, chauvinists, men obsessed with their last girlfriends, men obsessed with their last girlfriend's new boyfriend, needy guys, flirts, gropers, girly boys—"

"Basta!" Martha put out her cigarette. "The real problem is men don't know how to be good men anymore." She walked

over to the windows and looked across the garden courtyard to the opposite ivy-covered wall of the Kingston, where her own apartment was. "They've forgotten how to seduce women," she said, twisting a lock of hair. "Does that ever happen in nature? I mean, do male birds ever just forget to sing the songs that attract females?"

Lucy considered the question. "I've never come across it in my research."

"Simon wasn't a horrible person, just a horrible date," Martha continued, turning back to face Lucy. "You know, I think I could actually help them."

"Help them?" Lucy furrowed her brow in mock contemplation. "Let's see: Feed starving children, save the whales, or help incompetent men?"

"I'm serious. They can probably be taught."

"Taught what? How to be better men? You're proposing dating classes?"

"More like private tutorials," Martha said. "We go out on a date, and afterwards, I tell him what he's doing wrong. Or right." She closed her eyes and imagined what she would have said on her date last night: *Ask more questions, Simon. Don't try so hard to impress. Talk less. Relax.* In her fantasy, Simon is all smiles and nods. "Plus," she said, opening her eyes wide, "I bet it could be lucrative."

From that conversation, the concept for FirstDate was born. Lucy skipped her yoga class and brainstormed with Martha all day. *What would FirstDate's mission be?* To help men make more favorable impressions on their dates. *How would it work?* Clients would take Martha out to dinner as if it were a real first date and Martha would critique their courtship skills and tell them how to improve. *What would it cost?* A flat fee, plus the price of the meal. *Why would men do it?* The promise of results!

For the next two months, Martha dove headlong into her research. Of course, the anecdotal evidence from women overwhelmingly supported the need for FirstDate, but did men know they needed help? Would they pay for it? By and large, Martha's straight male friends refused to discuss it with her. When she asked her brother, Jesse, he suggested that Martha go back into therapy. And Lucy's normally unflappable boyfriend, Adam, got flustered just trying to explain all that was offensive about the concept.

But Martha was neither discouraged nor dissuaded. And sexist or not, Lucy believed that if men thought it would improve their chances with women, they'd sign up for FirstDate in droves. She cited a recent study, which demonstrated that male howler monkeys actively sought to learn new courtship behaviors that gave them competitive reproductive advantage over other males. "I don't see why it wouldn't be the same with humans," Lucy concluded.

Martha made the monkey-to-man leap. She developed a business plan, wrote a mission statement, and designed a Web site. Her only real outlay of cash came when she placed a couple of strategic advertisements in *New York* magazine and *Time Out New York,* as well as on local Internet dating sites. The ad read: MEN: YOU ONLY GET TO MAKE A FIRST IMPRESSION ONCE. HONE YOUR COURTSHIP SKILLS WITH FIRSTDATE.

AT LA LUNA, Lucy and Eva are dying to hear how Martha's first FirstDate went, but the actress in Martha wants her audience even hungrier. "Don't you just hate that you can't smoke in bars anymore?" she says.

"Out with it, girl. I've got a room full of thirsty customers," Eva says. "Who was your first guinea pig?"

"Come on," Lucy says impatiently.

"Okay, okay!" Martha says, but still pauses several beats. "Ladies, I have found my calling!"

Lucy raises her glass to make a toast and Eva mimes the same. "To FirstDate," she cheers and the three of them clink glasses, real and pretend.

"That's right," Martha says. "No more temping. No more waitressing. I've already got more than a week of FirstDates scheduled and I haven't even opened all the e-mails yet. Not only have I struck a chord in the collective subconscious of men, they're actually willing to admit they need help."

"And pay for it," Lucy adds.

"They want sex, for Christ's sake!" Eva says. "The fact that men are willing to humiliate themselves for it is hardly news."

Martha shushes Eva but is momentarily distracted by the sandy-haired man who smiles at her from across the bar. "He's kind of cute, don't you think?"

"Take my word, you're not interested," Lucy says. "Now, date details please!"

"Okay," Martha continues. "The stats: Jake Stevens, photojournalist, around forty, short, nice eyes—except they're focused to the side of my head. I mean, he makes no eye contact. At one point, I turn around to see if there's a cockroach crawling up the wall or pinup calendar. What could possibly hold his undivided interest like that? But there's nothing. So I get down to business and ask him what he thinks his dating issues are. Without skipping a beat he says, 'I probably just haven't met the right woman yet.' "

"Yeah, Jake, that's probably it," Eva snorts.

"My first thought is, Oh my God, they're all going to say that." Martha stops. "Then I think of how many times I've said it myself."

Lucy takes a sip of wine. "This is humbling work, Martha. Noble and humbling."

"Next, I notice that Jake's hands are trembling—I mean really trembling—and I'm thinking, Um, isn't that sort of a problem for a photojournalist?"

"Maybe he's just nervous to be on a date," Lucy says.

Eva shakes a martini. "As opposed to how he feels taking pictures in war-torn wherever."

"Well, I have to admit I was nervous, too," Martha says. "But I just treated it like stage fright and got into character. Remember that nurse I played on *All My Children*?"

"Sure," Lucy says. "You were good."

"I was *great*," Martha says, clearly still riding high on the adrenaline wave of the evening. "With Jake I became the empathetic and highly efficient Nurse Joanne all over again. And it worked. I said to Jake: 'Here's the deal. For the first ten minutes, I'll ask you questions; after that, we pretend it's a real date.' Then I asked him all the questions we came up with—what are his dating fears, what type of woman does he want to meet, blah, blah, blah."

"And you told him the rules?" Lucy asks.

"No kissing, no second dates, and, once the date starts, no questions of the how-am-I-doing variety. We'll go over everything in the debriefing."

"Cool," Lucy says. "And how'd phase two go?"

"That's where things got tricky. When we left the bar, Jake took me to Yak-Yak."

"Yak-Yak?"

"A Tibetan restaurant in the East Village. Four tables. No

chairs. Cushions on the floor. It was by the grace of God that I'd decided not to wear my pencil skirt. I'd have never made it down. Anyway, Jake is talking so quietly"—Martha lowers her own voice—"I have to lean over the table to hear him. I say, 'Excuse me?' and he tells me he's a Buddhist and would like to meditate for a few minutes before dinner. Next thing I know, he's *ohm*ing away."

"Jesus," Eva says.

"What did you do?" Lucy asks.

"What could I do?" Martha replies. "But whether it's Buddhism or Yak-Yak, something suddenly starts working for Jake. His hands stop shaking and he gets all serene, sitting cross-legged on his pillow. In fact, he's so Zenned out that I start to feel like I'm intruding on what has become *his* date."

Martha turns to Eva: "Ask me about the wine list."

Before Eva can get the words out, Martha plunges on. "No wine. No beer. No nothing. Can you imagine?"

"Heart surgery without anesthesia," Eva says.

"Jake tells me to try the tea with yak butter. 'It's delicious,' he says."

"Why even bother trying to help men?" Eva asks, refilling Martha's glass. "Men are men, and even *you* won't be able to change them."

"Now don't start down that road again," Martha says. "You're becoming a cliché: the beautiful man-hating lesbian."

Eva mouths the word *beautiful* back to Lucy and basks in the compliment. Then she leans over the bar, resting on her elbows so that her breasts are sandwiched between her biceps and addresses both women: "Humor me. Think of the best man you know, picture how smart and good he is, remember the kindest thing he's done for you, the funniest joke he's ever told."

Martha imagines her younger brother, Jesse, and Lucy thinks

of her boyfriend, Adam. Both women smile.

"Now, compare those men with the best women you know."

Lucy and Martha hear the jaws of Eva's trap slam shut.

"You see? Even the best man you know only makes a so-so woman," Eva says. "Am I right?"

Lucy swivels on her stool to face Martha. "So how was the tea with yak butter?"

Martha crinkles her nose. "Just as greasy and gross as it sounds. I only took one swallow. I mean, who in his right mind takes a first date to a vegetarian restaurant that serves no booze unless he's squared it with her in advance?"

Lucy sighs. "Someone passive-aggressive?"

"More like Buddhist-aggressive," Martha says. "But you know what? The beauty of FirstDate is that at our follow-up meeting tomorrow, I get to send Jake off on the path of dating enlightenment and start anew. Now, enough about me, already. Spotlight on you!" She points to Lucy's magazine. "What animal porn are you reading tonight?"

Lucy looks at her *Biology Today.* "The usual stuff: all the ridiculous things males do to win females."

"Ah, yes. My favorite topic. Go on."

Lucy smiles. "This one is about a type of swallow that grows extremely long tail feathers to impress the ladies. And yet, the added weight can keep him from getting off the ground."

"Seems like a small sacrifice to make," Martha says, eyeing a man who doesn't help his date with her coat.

"It's not, though," Lucy says. "Some of these males literally can't fly, never mind helping with the nest-work."

"Let me get this right: In order to get the girl, the boy incapacitates himself?" Martha asks, thinking, *That's so sweet.*

"Like women who wear stilettos," Eva sneers, managing to serve the rest of her customers and still catch most of their conversation.

"In nature, the rules are reversed," Lucy says. "Males must please females, no matter the cost."

"So what's in it for the girl if her guy can't build a nest?" Martha asks.

"Think George Clooney. Would it bother you if he couldn't patch the roof?"

"Point taken."

"In the end, it all depends on what females need males for. In species where males help with domestic matters, females select based on domestic skills; in species where they don't," Lucy points to her magazine article, "females select according to aesthetic preferences. But in both cases, the males are always the seducers. They do whatever it takes—whether that means butting heads, fanning feathers, or flying loop-de-loops—to attract a mate."

"So why are human men so hopeless in courtship?" Martha asks.

Lucy shrugs. "No idea."

"But Adam seduced you, didn't he?"

Good question, Lucy thinks back. Had Adam seduced her? Not really. She'd noticed him first, hunched over some economics book in the library. Then she'd switched cubicles to get a little closer. When she got a good look at his soulful brown eyes, she'd made a point of saying hello. "Now that I think about it, I'm not so sure," she admits.

"Well, who asked who to dinner the first time?"

Lucy hesitates. "I think it was one of those impromptu grab-a-bite-after-work things."

"Who kissed who first?" Eva asks. "I know you remember that!"

Silence. "Well, Adam did kiss me, but I think I might have

said something to encourage him."

"Something like: 'Hurry up and kiss me, already?' " Eva adds.

Martha glares at her, but Eva doesn't back down. Her look says, *See, I told you, even the best men are lacking!*

"Actually, Eva's right," admits Lucy.

"Who cares?" Martha says, sensing she's hit a nerve. "What's important is that you're together now. You two love each other and that's all that matters."

"I guess so," Lucy says, but her voice gets small. "Spotlight back on you. Seems to me someone has to find a legit date in the next ten days or risk the consequences of a failed New Year's resolution."

"What are the consequences again?" Martha asks.

"Dinner at the restaurant of my choice, which could get expensive once a month for a whole year," Lucy says. "Besides, you promised you'd try."

CHAPTER 2

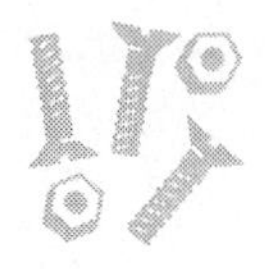

"I love the idea of two sexes, don't you?"

James Thurber

THE COST TO Martha for breaking her New Year's resolution and not going out on a date in January is dinner for two at a pricy sushi bar in the West Village, where Lucy orders every delicacy she can think of—sea urchin with quail egg, fatty tuna, baby yellowtail, giant sea clam—on the assumption that a little financial squeeze will help persuade her friend to find a date in February. Lucy puts a piece of ginger on top of the last glistening slab of fish, dunks it in soy sauce, and pops it in her mouth. A moment later, she reaches for the menu. "Anything else for you?"

"I know what you're doing and it's not going to work," Martha says. "You're forgetting that money is no longer an issue. I had four FirstDates last week, so eat until you burst."

Lucy sighs and orders a pot of green tea instead. "How were those dates anyway? Any more religious fanatics?"

Martha shakes her head. "They were a peculiar bunch, all strangely nonmasculine. You know the type I mean? Good-looking, immaculately dressed, very witty, but with zero sexual vibe. Yet supposedly straight."

"Exactly the kind of man you don't want to be stranded on a desert island with, right?"

Martha nods and is silent for a moment. "Here's a question for the biologist in you: If these femmy straight guys don't know how to seduce women, aren't they bound for extinction?"

"Only time will tell, I guess," Lucy says, thinking of Adam, who's gentle and cerebral, and arguably not a paragon of masculinity.

"Why is it that so many guys today don't seem to know how to do basic man stuff? How have we lost that in a single generation?" Martha tries to think if she's ever had a handy boyfriend. "All of our fathers knew how to repair things, yet no man within ten years of our age does. What do you do when something breaks around your apartment?"

"The little things I take care of myself," Lucy says. "For the complicated stuff, I wait for Cooper's visits. Last time he was in town, he rewired a lamp, fixed my vacuum cleaner, and built shelves in my bedroom closet for my shoes."

"Ah, that Cooper," Martha says, thinking of Lucy's best friend from college. "What do you think accounts for the difference in him? How does he know how to do everything?"

"Growing up on a dairy farm had to have helped. It wasn't as if the Tuckingtons could call the superintendent every time something broke," Lucy says. "Cooper's just so capable and resourceful, he could survive in the woods for weeks with only a penknife. But he's also polite in the way men from our father's generation are. He holds doors and carries things, and it never feels patronizing. It feels natural."

"And as I recall, he's also big and handsome and strong," Martha says, smiling. "Now remind me again why you two never hooked up?"

Lucy recollects the huge crush she had on Cooper when he was her residence counselor freshman year. "Oh, you know. In the beginning, one or the other of us was always involved with someone and then we just got to know each other too well to date."

"What does that mean, exactly?"

"It means the man drinks Coke with breakfast, for God's sake, and reads the last page of a novel first."

And the problem with that would be? Martha wonders.

Lucy takes a sip of tea. "We do have the Pact, of course," she says, referring to their promise to be each other's backup if neither was married by the time Lucy turned thirty. Four years ago (on Lucy's twenty-ninth birthday), they upped it to thirty-five.

The last of Martha's backups got married years ago. "At the risk of sounding like a snob, how does a Columbia graduate end up a dairy farmer?"

Lucy had asked Cooper the same question a dozen times in college. "If he were here, he'd challenge you to explain why the lessons of literature and philosophy are more germane to your life than his," she says, picturing Cooper milking cows at dawn with a copy of Nietzsche's *Beyond Good and Evil* in his back pocket.

"I guess he has a point. It's not as if my psychology degree has done a whole lot for my acting career," Martha says, applying a perfect coat of bloodred lipstick. "So, do you have any plans after dinner?"

"An article on the monogamous nature of the California mouse and bed," Lucy replies.

"You mean all mice aren't rats? And here I've been looking

for a man when all I really need is a mouse!" Martha shakes her head. "Why don't you come over for a nightcap? I'm meeting Jesse at my apartment in a half hour. He's going to help me put up a shelf."

"Put up a shelf?" Lucy says. Her tone implies the rest: *Your brother? Carpentry? Are you kidding?*

"Tread lightly, Luce. We're talking about my gene pool."

"I just had no idea he was even remotely handy."

"Well, I'll have to let you know tomorrow if you're going to pass up a ringside seat."

"Hey," Lucy says, as Martha gets ready to leave. "Let's not forget the purpose of our little meal tonight."

"To punish me for not having a date?"

"Not punish, Martha. I'm on your side. Can't we at least try to discuss why you've been such a hermit lately?"

Martha shrugs. "I've been busy," she says, sinking back into the chair and wrapping her cardigan tightly around herself. "I don't know, Luce, it feels too hard. Besides, I was dating in January. Sort of."

"FirstDates don't count."

Martha shrugs again.

"Who was the last guy you went out on a *real* date with?"

"Simon Hodges."

"The political historian who nearly bored you to death? That was months ago."

"What can I say? Simon was the straw that broke this camel's back. I don't even know why. He didn't do anything terrible, but part of me just gave up after him."

"Gave up what?"

"All hope?" Martha forces out an unconvincing laugh.

"Oh, Martha. I know it's hard," Lucy says. "But maybe you could just pretend that every date you go on is a story you can tell me later. The bad ones will be hilarious and, eventually, there'll be a good one. I was about to give up when I met Adam, remember?"

Martha makes an effort to smile, but it fades almost immediately. "I just wish my mother felt the same way."

"What did she do this time?"

"Nothing really. Her attitude has shifted, though." Martha fills her mug with tea. "After a lifetime of telling me that no man is good enough—this one's forehead slopes, that one doesn't make enough money, he drinks too much, and so on—suddenly Mom's panicking. She used to worry that I'd settle for someone beneath me. Now she's worried that no one will settle for *me.*"

"That's crazy."

"Yesterday she called to tell me that I shouldn't feel like I've totally missed my chance at marriage. 'There are still widowers,' she said."

"No!"

"I swear, Luce, if I brought home a Neanderthal tomorrow, my mother would tell me just how charming knuckle-dragging can be."

Lucy pictures Martha's mother, Betsy, in action. An inveterate hostess, Betsy approaches motherhood with the detached politeness of a flight attendant. She treats her daughter like a first-class passenger, making sure she's comfortable and well fed, and always keeps the conversation breezy.

"She actually suggested that I go out with Stanley."

"As in the neighbor's son who thinks he's writing the Great American Novel and still lives at home at the age of forty?" Lucy asks. "*That* Stanley?"

"That Stanley."

Lucy takes off her glasses and rubs the bridge of her nose. "Don't take this the wrong way, but if there's one thing that your mother's good for, it's making me feel slightly better about my own."

"I feel exactly the same way about your mom." Martha laughs. "Virginia scares the hell out of me."

"My mom *is* scary," Lucy says, "but at least she's still in the no-man-is-good-enough-for-me camp. Of course, that includes Adam." Lucy sighs. "I get so tired of her trashing him. It's as if she wants me to doubt him."

"She probably does. That way you depend on her more, right?"

"Exactly. But as much as I try to ignore her, what she says seeps into my head. Then, when Adam does something annoying, I hear her voice coming out of my mouth."

"Oh God. The dreaded realization that you're turning into your mother," Martha says.

"Lately, Mom likes to ask if I find Adam *interesting,*" Lucy says, imitating the way her mother drags out the word. "What she really means by that is that Adam doesn't make *her* feel interesting."

"I don't get it," Martha says. "Adam's supposed to laugh more at her jokes?"

"No, that would mean he has a wonderful sense of humor," Lucy explains. "To be *interesting,* he must hang on her every word."

"Poor Adam. He's no match for Virginia." Martha signals for the check. "How's he doing, anyway?"

"He's *okay,*" Lucy says, but her voice lingers on all that's mediocre in the word.

"What's going on?"

"He didn't get the fellowship he was hoping for, so he has to TA again this semester: Freshman Economics 101. I think he's discouraged. And possibly humiliated."

Martha imagines that having a girlfriend who's the rising superstar in her department can't make things easier. "How are you feeling about him these days?" she asks.

"I'd be lying if I told you I wasn't having my doubts," Lucy says. "Adam drags his insecurity around with him like it's mud on his shoes, and I want to scream, 'Don't track that shit in here!' "

Martha almost laughs, but sees how serious Lucy is.

"I don't know how often a guy can tell you that he isn't worthy of you before some part of you starts to believe it. What's worse is, I think it's changing the way he feels about me, too." Lucy's eyes start to water and she looks up, blinking.

"Are you crazy?" Martha asks. "The man leaves Post-it love notes all over your apartment, for God's sake. He might be going through a rough time, but he's not backing off." She puts her hand on Lucy's. "You guys still going away over Valentine's Day?"

Lucy nods, brightening at the thought of the rustic, yellow farmhouse her colleagues, the Wolfs, are loaning them for a long weekend. The house is two hours up the Hudson and she and Adam will spend four days in the woods with only a Franklin stove to cook on.

"My idea of hell," Martha says. She flips over the check and her eyes widen. "Lucy Stone, I hope you feel guilty making your poor spinster friend pay for her spinsterhood." She slaps down a credit card and looks at her watch. She was supposed to meet Jesse ten minutes ago.

MARTHA HEARS *LA BOHÈME* blaring in the hallway before she even reaches her apartment door and feels inexplicably annoyed that Jesse has brought his own music. Is hers all that bad? Her brother's love of opera started at the age of fourteen (a particularly inopportune moment in a boy's life to develop such a passion), while Martha was at Boston College. At the time, she cursed her parents' influence and did her best to intervene, sending Jesse tapes of Nirvana, Pearl Jam, and R.E.M. None of them had the intended effect.

Martha turns the key, but her door won't open. She tries again, this time jiggling the lock, but still nothing. Then it occurs to her that her nervous brother has dead-bolted it from the inside. She pounds on the door and calls his name, but the music is too loud for him to hear her. She wonders whom exactly he thinks he's keeping out, but Jesse's been high-strung his whole life.

Martha goes down to the concierge and gets her spare key. As soon as she walks into her apartment, she hits the eject button on her CD player and the machine spits out *La Bohème* and swallows up Bob Marley. She calms herself by practicing a square breathing technique an acting coach taught her: in on four, hold for four, out on four, hold for four. Immediately she feels better, listening to "No Woman, No Cry," anticipating her first glass of wine and glancing around her apartment, which feels more like a lounge with its plush velvet sofas, dim lighting, and ever-present smell of cigarette smoke. "It's all about mood," Martha explained to Lucy the first time she visited after they met in the Kingston's laundry room five years ago.

Lucy dubbed the apartment the Bordello, a name Martha protests but secretly loves.

In a better frame of mind now, Martha moseys into the kitchen to greet her brother, swaying to the beat of the reggae. "Hey, larvae," she says. "Don't you think it's a tad excessive to bolt the top lock?"

"Don't you think it's a tad rude to be half an hour late when I'm here to do you a favor?"

Jesse has a slender six-foot frame with nice shoulders and an angular face not unlike Martha's, only his chin ends in a deep cleft and there's no gray in his curly hair, which he wears neatly parted on the side, glued down with a little too much styling gel. He's in his casual clothes—creased blue jeans and a perfectly pressed white oxford.

Martha apologizes. "I'm a little stressed out from my conversation with Lucy." When Jesse doesn't ask about it, she says, "We talked about the sorry-ass state of men in New York."

Jesse mumbles something sympathetic and goes back to doing what he was doing when she got there: searching through his small toolbox.

"Need help?" Martha asks. "Or should I just stick to pouring wine?"

"I'm okay. Just having a little trouble finding my screws." He peers into the orderly, wooden box. "They should be in the *S*-through-*Z* section."

He didn't just say that, Martha thinks, squeezing past him to get to the refrigerator. "White okay?" she asks. It's all she has. Then she can't stop herself: "Your tools are *alphabetized*?"

Ignoring her, Jesse begins elaborately washing his hands, soaping from his fingertips to his wrists and back. When he's done, he holds his hands up surgeon-style and scans the room for something to dry them with. He rules out a germy dish towel, opting instead for a paper napkin. "Where do you want the shelf to go?"

Martha points to a spot above the sink. "There. Basically, I want to be able to put my cookbooks on it, and maybe a vase or two. What do you think?"

"Perfect," he says, nodding with confidence, which for some

reason makes Martha nervous.

"Don't forget to use wall anchors," she says, picturing the ugly holes Jesse seems about to inflict on her walls.

"What?"

"Wall anchors. You know what they are, don't you?"

"M-a-r-t-h-a," Jesse says, stretching her name into a warning.

"What? I can't ask a question?"

Jesse picks up the little kitchen stool Martha uses to reach the bowls and platters that are stored on top of her cabinets and places it at the far end of the kitchen. "Sit down, drink your wine, and no backseat carpentry."

"Fair enough," she says, and does as she's told. The wine-glass is cool in her hands and she takes a large swallow, resigning her shelf and her wall to their fates. "So, what's up in the world of editing children's books?"

"I've discovered two wonderful new writers," he says, rising up onto his toes in excitement.

Martha makes a mental note to discuss his tiptoeing habit with him at some point.

Jesse fills her in on his latest book acquisitions, *Chicken Bedtime Is Early* and *Wheezy Weed Gets Whacked.* His face is animated as he describes the stories, their illustrations, and the children the books will appeal to, and Martha is reminded how much her brother loves his work. She only wishes that the rest of his life were as easy. Jesse is wound too tightly. He leaps when trucks drive over manholes and he worries constantly about germ warfare; anxiety attacks keep him up at night and allergies bother him during the day; the skin on his hands is chapped from over-washing and the prolific use of antibacterial wipes. Recently, he bought four identical pairs of shatter-proof eye glasses.

"What about that woman you told me about? How's that going?" Martha asks.

"Andrea?" Jesse says with a shy smile. "We had our third date last night."

"And?"

"I think it's going pretty well," he says, putting in the third of six screws along a line he's drawn on the wall. Plaster and paint chips and dust crumble out with each twist.

Martha wants to avert her eyes, but can't make herself. *Listen to what your brother is saying, don't look at what he's destroying.* "Any canoodling to report?"

Jesse blushes. "Andrea hasn't given me very clear signs."

Martha notices that the line he's penciled onto the wall slopes downward. "Don't you think agreeing to a third date is a clear signal?"

"I guess I was hoping she'd let me know if she wanted to, uh, be kissed."

Martha rolls her eyes. "Why's that her job?"

Jesse looks at his sister. "Well, it's not her job per se, but I don't want to be offensive or overly aggressive." He resumes his work. "Andrea is just so smart and capable and independent that I figure she'll let me know when she's ready to step things up."

This is what Andrea gets for being smart, capable, and independent! Martha thinks. "There's nothing offensive about letting her know how you feel."

Jesse loses his grip and the screwdriver slips from its groove and out of his hand, skittering across the kitchen counter and landing on the floor. "How about some help?" Together they pick up the shelf, guide the six loop fixtures over the six screws, and lower it into place.

"Do you know how I'd like to be treated by a man?" Martha asks.

"With respect?" Jesse says hopefully. He tightens the screws, oblivious to the shelf's slant.

"Yes, of course, but I also want to be pursued and courted and seduced."

A look of discomfort crosses Jesse's face.

"How about letting your natural alpha-male instincts come out a little with Andrea?" Martha suggests.

Jesse starts to hum "Toreador" from his favorite opera, *Carmen,* and Martha can tell from his faraway look that he's testing his alpha-male instincts by imagining he's a charging bull about to confront a matador. He's standing tall with his chest thrust forward and his shoulders square.

"Da dum da dum dum da de da de dum," he sings until he stops abruptly and his shoulders slump.

"What happened, Toreador?" Martha asks.

Jesse looks at his sister. "I started thinking about Ferdinand."

Ferdinand the Bull is the story of a sweet bull who's mistakenly thought to be fierce when matadors see him bucking wildly after a bee sting. They cart him off to a bullring in Madrid, where he's expected to fight, but all Ferdinand does is admire the flowers that decorate the ladies' hats. It's Jesse's favorite book from childhood.

"Look, Martha, you know as well as I do that I was raised to be a nice Catholic boy. Plus, I've had to listen to you for thirty-plus years and I've dated New York women for the last twelve. As a result, any alpha-male instinct I had has either been bred or beaten out of me."

"But don't you sometimes want to completely ravish Andrea?"

"Ravish?" Jesse couldn't sound more shocked if Martha had suggested slipping Andrea a Spanish fly. "You're the one who trained me to be sensitive, remember?"

"I know I did. Sorry."

"You're freaking me out here."

Martha stands up. "It's a disaster!"

Jesse looks at his handiwork.

"Not the shelf. You and Andrea! You can't expect her do all the work." Martha strides into the living room. "Think of how courtship works in nature: males strut and fight and sing their little hearts out to get females. Ask Lucy."

Jesse closes his toolbox and follows her out.

"Why don't you kiss Andrea tonight?" Martha asks. "Just call her right now and tell her you can't stop thinking about her."

A loud *meow* interrupts them and gives Jesse the out he needs. "I have to go," he says, gathering his belongings. "I locked psycho kitty in the bathroom." He folds his scarf carefully over his chest, leaving one end free to place discreetly over his nose and mouth should he need to protect himself from coughing passengers on the bus.

Martha hands him his coat and kisses his cheek. "Thanks for the help."

"Glad to do it." Jesse puts on his hat and pulls down the earflaps, just like a six-year-old might.

Martha hopes that if he does muster the courage to see Andrea tonight, he'll take off the hat.

Once Jesse leaves, Martha opens the bathroom door and her orange tabby, Hannibal, shoots out and begins to circle her ankles, madly rubbing and purring and mewing, simultaneously demanding to be fed and petted. The cat might be one of Jesse's few justifiable fears. Hannibal ambushes the ankles of anyone other than Martha who enters the Bordello.

"Is it any wonder no man will spend the night with me with you here?" she asks Hannibal, as she pours kibbles into his bowl. Martha studies her brother's handiwork and very gingerly places

The Joy of Cooking on the slanted shelf.

CHAPTER 3

"Men lose more conquests by their own awkwardness than by any virtue in the woman."

Ninon de Lenclos

MATCHES, COMPASS, CANDLES, wool socks, red wine, snow boots, bird book. As Lucy makes a mental list of what she and Adam will need for their weekend in the woods, her brow furrows. *Call Hertz. Get map of Ulster County. Bake cookies. Bring corkscrew.* Unable to keep track of it all, she grabs a legal pad and scribbles down her questions: *Should we bring water? Wood? Supplies for outhouse? Kerosene for lamps? First aid kit?* Her stress level grows proportionally to the list and before she realizes what she's doing, her fingers are tapping Cooper's number onto the phone pad. His answering machine picks up.

"Cooper? Are you there? It's me." She pauses for a moment, stepping over a pile of supplies for the trip: hiking boots, strike-anywhere matches, long underwear. "Okay. I guess you're not in. Call me back. Today, if possible. We're going upstate this weekend to a friend's farmhouse that has no running water, no electricity, only a woodstove—"

"Hey, Lucy-goose," Cooper says, slightly out of breath when he finally picks up. "I was out back working on my truck. Now, what's got your feathers in a ruffle?"

All at once her feathers settle and she feels silly for being nervous in the first place. "Hey, Coop," she says. "How's everything down there?"

"Everything's grand, sweetheart."

"Why's it always so grand with you, anyway?"

"Visit someday and find out."

It's a running joke between them: in the twelve years since they've known each other, Lucy's never been to Tuckington Farm.

"Yeah, I know. I'd be a sweeter, happier person if I woke up to cows mooing instead of horns honking," Lucy says. "But I think you grossly underestimate the competitive edge that crankiness gives a city girl."

"Perhaps I do," he says. "Maybe I should come up and suss out the situation in person."

"Oh, why don't you, Cooper? Your annual visit is long overdue."

"You're right about that. And I could sure use a break about now."

"Mi casa es su casa," Lucy says.

"Well, maybe I'll look into flights later in the week. But first things first. How can I help with this *terrifying* trip into the savage wilderness of upstate New York?"

Lucy ignores his teasing and starts right in with her questions: "There's some kind of a siphon system that transports water from the well to the house through hoses. Have you ever used one?"

"Sure. They're temperamental," Cooper says, all business now. "You might want to bring a few gallons of water with you, especially if you plan to arrive at night and it's cold. You don't want to mess with frozen hoses."

She adds *water* to her list. "What about firewood? Should we buy some?"

"I guarantee your friends have a well-stocked woodpile," he says, and reassures her that small houses are easy to heat.

"But what if the logs are wet?" Lucy persists. "What do we do then?" Suddenly nervous again, she reads off her entire list in one frantic breath.

"It's only a weekend, Luce, but if you're so worried, maybe you and Martha shouldn't go it alone."

"Martha? I'm going with Adam. Friday is Valentine's Day." She hears a muffled sound on the other end, and realizes Cooper is laughing. "What exactly is so funny?"

"Just what a little worrier you are. Good God! You're going to suck the romance right out of this weekend if you don't relax."

"What do you mean?"

"Listen, Luce, Adam can handle this stuff. In fact, you need to let him handle it. Your questions are right out of the Boy Scout manual."

Lucy sifts through her memory to see if she can recall Adam ever mentioning building a campfire, whittling a stick, or partaking in any Boy Scout–like rituals. She's sure he's had no such training. What Adam's good at is abstract thinking, advanced mathematics, and the occasional love note. Not wilderness survival.

"You Yankee girls need to learn how to let men be men," Cooper says.

THE WIND IS GUSTING, and tiny, dry snowflakes swirl around the Hertz rental garage on West Thirty-fourth Street, where Adam and Lucy rendezvous for their weekend. It's a blustery day and they're bundled up, Lucy looking ready for the Iditarod, in a blue down parka with a fur-trimmed hood, and Adam in his heavy, navy peacoat, with a gray wool hat and scarf set that his mother gave him for Christmas.

Adam says hello to the small patch of Lucy's face that's visible and kisses her pink nose. As planned, they arrive at the rental office at noon to eliminate any chance that they won't find the Wolfs' farmhouse by dark.

Lucy takes the first shift behind the wheel, trying not to be annoyed that Adam forgot his driver's license.

"I remembered the flashlight you told me to bring," he says, as if the one makes up for the other.

Lucy gives him her best, no-problem smile and steps on the gas. There's no traffic and they speed up the Westside Highway, over the George Washington Bridge, and along the Palisades Parkway, where she and Adam get intermittent peeks of the ice-covered Hudson River, which has a path cut through the center so that boats can pass. Excited to be going away with Adam, Lucy tears along the highway, maneuvering in and out of lanes and between cars with the grace of a professional hockey player.

Adam's right hand never leaves the dashboard.

Near Bear Mountain, they stop at a scenic overlook to eat a couple of turkey and Brie sandwiches Lucy packed.

"Have I told you recently that you make the best sandwiches in the world?" Adam says, chomping into his, the corners of his mouth shiny with mayonnaise.

"No," Lucy lies. She loves that Adam thinks she's a wonderful cook.

The flurries have stopped for a moment and, in the distance, Lucy sees a pair of bald eagles leaving an aerie on the other side of the river. She points them out to Adam. "Aren't they beautiful?" she says, holding his hand. Whatever lapse of confidence she's been feeling about their relationship is buoyed by the sight of the birds. "They're kind of like people, you know. Eagles mate for life."

"That might be the least scientific thing I've ever heard you say," Adam replies.

Lucy wonders if this comment is meant to bring her down a peg professionally or personally. It smarts on both fronts and she tries not to sound hurt when she says, "I wasn't making a scientific observation."

"I'm sorry. I didn't mean for that to come out the way it did. It was supposed to be a joke." Adam looks genuinely contrite, but the mood has changed. They eat their sandwiches in silence for a few moments until he asks if she's read an article in the current issue of *Nature*. "It's about a new genetic fingerprinting technique that tracks birds. It's on your side of the bed."

Lucy shakes her head. There are stacks and stacks of biology magazines all over her apartment; she's forever trying to catch up.

"The new technique proves that only ten percent of birds that biologists used to believe mated for life are actually monogamous."

Lucy's stomach twists into a knot. *What's Adam's point?* She wishes she'd never mentioned the bald eagles and turns on the ignition. "Actually, how about you take over for a while?" She leaves the engine running, opens the door, and walks around to the other side.

When Adam's been driving for about fifteen minutes, Lucy

is struck by the realization that she's never seen him drive before. How New York is that? she thinks, and scrolls through the trips they've taken in their two years of coupledom: a week in Paris; no car was necessary. A Christmas vacation on Cape Cod; she drove her mother's. Several brief escapes to the Hamptons; they were given rides by friends. A couple of business trips; they took trains.

Lucy watches as towns pass by her window: Newburg, Marlboro, Highland, New Paltz. She's mesmerized by the swirling snow, which is getting wetter and heavier as they travel north. In this dreamy state, she imagines that they're already at the yellow farmhouse, sipping red wine in front of a roaring fire tended by a shirtless Adam. Just as she's about to stroke Fantasy Adam's well-muscled side, Real Adam hits the brakes and Lucy lurches forward, her seat belt catching her, as it has several times in the last twenty miles. She feels a wave of nausea from listing back and forth, and remembers Martha once telling her that everything you need to know about a man can be gleaned from how he drives: Is he confident? Self-centered? Reckless? Lucy wonders what to make of Adam's indecisive foot on the gas pedal—on/off, on/off, on/off—and tries not to draw any conclusions. She does, however, grow to dread every on-ramp and merge, where only after a series of jerky hesitations is Adam able to insert himself into the flow of traffic, much to the aggravation of the drivers around him.

Straining to cling to the shirtless, fire-tending vision of Adam, Lucy puts on her sexiest voice. "What's the first thing you want to do when we get to the farmhouse?"

Adam doesn't even glance Lucy's way; he's leaning forward, gripping the wheel. "At this point, my only concern is making it there in one piece."

The snow gets heavier as they near the Catskills. They get

lost on some of the smaller roads, passing old houses, dilapidated barns, country stores, and a ramshackle tavern with a neon BUD LIGHT sign in the window. Neglected stone walls, built hundreds of years ago, resemble long, crooked smiles with missing teeth. Friendly, earnest signs give directions to local ski areas, recommend restaurants, offer solutions to legal problems. There's even one with three smiling tomatoes kicking up little stick legs Rockette-style over the message: LOCALLY GROWN, LOCALLY KNOWN. Utterly charmed, Lucy's ready to move to Ulster County.

When they pull into the driveway, Lucy gasps with delight. The yellow farmhouse sits at the edge of a large meadow that is dwarfed by hills on the other side. For a moment she just takes it in, then she unbuckles her seat belt and hugs Adam. "We're here!"

She leaves him to unpack the trunk while she gets the key, hidden beneath a stone in the window box. With a push and a creak, the front door opens into a musty-smelling cabin, with uneven floorboards and unfinished beams.

Adam traipses in after her, kicking the snow off his boots in a way that sounds like a complaint, but when Lucy turns around, she sees that he's carrying some holly branches.

"They're beautiful," she says, taking them from him and putting them in a large pitcher on the kitchen table. She rubs her hands together. "How about you start the fire and I unpack?"

The house is one large room. A denim futon that doubles as a sofa sits in front of the Franklin stove, and the skin of some extremely fuzzy animal lies on the floor in between. The rug looks incredibly soft, and Lucy wonders if they'll make love on it later. The kitchen area has an old farm table, a basin for a sink, and pots hanging from hooks on the clapboard wall.

"Don't you think it's adorable?" she asks.

"Adorable?" Adam takes in the Wolfs' odd assortment of antique tools propped against walls and hanging from beams: a two-tined pitchfork beside a dented shovel, an ax, a sledgehammer and wedge, a bow with horn tips and lots of arrows in a decaying quiver. "These look like props from a horror flick. And what the hell's that?" he asks, pointing to a metal device hanging from a hook on the wall.

Lucy examines the old animal trap, the kind that works on a spring and snaps shut on the animal's foot. There's a tiny bone, most likely a toe joint, suspended delicately between its metal jaws.

"Interesting," she says.

"More like gruesome."

Adam kneels down in front of the Franklin stove and Lucy watches him lay folded sections of the newspaper on the bottom of the hearth.

"Need any help?" she says, willing him to scrunch up the paper into balls, but remembering Cooper's admonition—*You Yankee girls need to let men be men*—she doesn't say a word.

"I'm fine."

Wine, Lucy thinks. A glass of wine will make everything okay. She opens the better of the two bottles she brought and finds a cupboard full of old Dundee Marmalade containers that apparently serve as mugs for all occasions. She fills one up and kneels down on the rug beside Adam, who's lighting the corners of the newspaper. She hands him the mug and, after he's taken a sip, wriggles into his arms and kisses him. "It's your job to keep me warm until this fire gets going," she says. They embrace and sink into the rug, kissing and moving against each other, until abruptly Adam pushes her off him. Smoke is spewing from the stove in great curlicues and the wood is smoldering without any flames.

"What the hell!" he says, leaping up.

"Did you open the flue?" Lucy asks.

Adam glares at her and drops to his knees, placing his head near the mouth of the stove so that he can see inside to find the lever.

Lucy finds it first, on the outside of the chimney pipe. "I got it," she says, flipping the lever so that the flue opens and the smoke starts to flow up and out. She tries to cozy up to Adam again, but he gets up and clomps across the room to open the door and clear out the remaining smoke. His heavy steps reverberate against the floor, causing a log to dislodge and roll onto the lip of the stove. While his back is turned, Lucy pushes the log back with the fire tongs and jams a few balls of crumpled newspaper underneath the wood so that the fire catches in earnest.

The house warms up quickly and they grill a London broil over the stove and bury two tinfoil-wrapped potatoes deep in the hot coals. They open a second bottle of wine and get slightly drunk as they feed each other dinner.

Before going to bed, they decide to brave the outhouse together, and though Adam did remember to bring the flashlight, he forgot to check the batteries, which are all but dead. The light casts no beam, making it useful only as a glow stick to announce their whereabouts to any hungry animals lurking in the dark. They huddle close together and trudge across the lawn, sinking shin-deep into the snow, neither admitting to being scared.

"Ladies first," Adam says, standing guard while Lucy ventures in.

The door shuts behind her and the outhouse—a glorified shed, really—is pitch black inside. Lucy imagines this might be a blessing, but it takes considerable willpower to pull down her pants and perch above what she knows is a numbingly cold seat. She shuts her eyes and concentrates by humming softly to herself. The wind howls and she hears branches snapping under the weight of the snow outside. Then she hears a louder sound, a *thunk,* and without warning, the door swings open and Adam leaps inside with her, stepping on her foot before landing solidly on his own.

"Jesus!" she says, standing and yanking up her pants.

"Sorry. Sorry." He turns his back to her.

"What's wrong?"

"There's something out there. I heard it in the woods." Adam's breathing is shallow and fast, and Lucy strains to hear what he's heard. All is quiet.

"Maybe it was just a big limb that fell," Lucy says, inching toward the door. "It's wet, heavy snow, that's for sure."

"Jesus, Lucy, it wasn't snow. Something's out there."

Lucy pushes open the door a crack, sees nothing. "Well, whatever it was, it's gone now. Want me to wait outside while you go?"

"Out there? Alone? Don't be ridiculous. I didn't really have to go anyway. Let's just get back to the house."

Adam steps in front of Lucy and sticks his head out the door, shining the dim flashlight into the darkness. He looks both ways before sprinting back to the farmhouse, not realizing Lucy isn't by his side until he reaches the front door. He waves for her to hurry up, but Lucy can't see him in the dark and walks back at her own pace.

"I really did hear something," he says when she gets to the door.

"I know you did, honey."

Adam locks the door behind them and announces that he's

going to bed. He climbs onto the futon without undressing and lies on his side, facing away from her. He closes his eyes and, in a few minutes, is fast asleep. Or pretending to be.

Lucy slowly takes off her shirt and swings it over the pitchfork. Surely, Adam is joking. She wriggles out of her jeans, unhooks her bra, and peels off her underwear, tossing it onto the bed. Nothing! Could he really be asleep? She can't decide whether to be mad or hurt, and slides under the covers beside him. She stares at the back of his neck where hair sprouts out from under his T-shirt and concentrates on how much she hates back hair.

—

Lucy wakes up early, cold and with a full bladder. Adam's head is partly under a pillow and he's pulled most of the blankets off her during the night. She slips into her long johns and tries to start a fire, crinkling up the sports section into neat balls and placing them on top of last night's ashes. She tosses on some kindling and three logs, which she arranges tepee-style, and soon the fire catches. She puts on a pot of water for coffee.

Still asleep, Adam looks angelic in the twisted sheets, and Lucy vows to make this a better day. One of his feet sticks out and she covers it with the blanket.

Adam stirs. "Morning," he says.

"Happy Valentine's Day."

"You, too. Sleep okay?"

She nods. "You?"

"Pretty well."

"I'm going to the outhouse. How about some coffee and a cuddle when I get back?"

"Sounds good. Want company?"

"I'll be fine," Lucy says.

Adam's smile vanishes and he rolls over onto his stomach.

When she returns, he's sitting on top of the folded-up bed.

"What about my coffee and cuddle?"

Adam hands her a Dundee mug full of hot coffee and pats the spot next to him on the sofa, as if being beside him is cuddle enough. His notebook is opened to a page of scribbled equations.

"Hey, no work on Valentine's Day," Lucy says, prying the notebook from his hands.

Adam looks perplexed. "Brain not warmed up. Need numbers to function."

"I'll give you numbers," Lucy says, raking her fingers through her blonde hair. "I'm going to teach you Valentine's Day math. One." She kisses him on the mouth once. "Two." Both eyelids. "Three." Cheek, nose, cheek. "Three times three." Nine rapid-fire kisses down his chest. "Warmed up yet?"

"Maybe a little," Adam says, coming around. "But you know I left simple arithmetic thirty years ago. I need the kiss equivalent of quantum chromodynamics."

"I can do that," Lucy says. And she does.

It's almost noon when they finish their breakfast and Lucy suggests that Adam find the well. They need to hook up the hoses to wash the dishes and themselves. He puts on his peacoat and dutifully trudges up the path with the Wolfs' directions in hand. He's gone for twenty minutes before Lucy pulls on her boots and ventures out after him, following his tracks into the woods and shouting his name.

"Over here," he calls back.

Lucy walks up a small hill toward his voice and finds Adam kneeling in the snow beside the well, which is partially covered by a piece of plywood. His gloves are off and his bare hands are red from the cold. He holds the hose in one hand and pours well water into it with the other, trying to create the vacuum needed to activate the siphon system, but it's not working.

"What's the matter?" Lucy asks.

Adam points to his leg, which is soaked. "I slipped when I was lifting off the plywood."

"Oh, honey."

"And I can't get this bloody thing to start." He lifts the end of the hose higher.

"You must be freezing," Lucy says, taking the hose and jug from his hands. "Why don't you let me take a stab at this and you go back to the house. If I can't do it, I'll be right behind you." She reads the handwritten instructions, which lie on a rock, and pours water into the funnel. As it gurgles into the hose, she plunges the end deep into the slushy well, which she desperately hopes will cause gravity to suck the water down the hill to the house.

Adam's hardly walked twenty feet by the time Lucy has the siphon system up and running. "You must have primed it for me," she says to him, as if he'd loosened the lid on a jelly jar. They don't say a word to each other as they walk down the hill; the snow is loud beneath their feet.

Back inside, Adam removes his wet jeans and long underwear, hanging them over the stovepipe to dry. His legs are skinny and goose-pimply, and he looks like an uncooked chicken, his penis dangling along his right thigh. He stands in front of the fire, now mostly orange embers, to warm up.

"I'm afraid that's the last of the chopped wood," Lucy says, scanning the Wolfs' note for the part about firewood, which she reads aloud: " 'Partially chopped tree in back. Use sledgehammer and wedge in corner by front door to split.' "

Adam pulls on a dry pair of boxers and jeans and grabs the sledgehammer and wedge. For weeks, his back has been giving him trouble and he struggles to close the door behind him with his hands full of the heavy iron equipment.

Lucy turns on the faucet and icy-cold water sputters into the basin. She fills a large kettle with enough water to do the dishes and lugs it to the stove to warm. When she returns to the sink, she looks out the window and watches Adam line up a couple of large logs to split. She loves the idea of him chopping wood and anticipates the delicious *thwack!* of the logs splitting.

Hunched over, Adam tentatively *tap tap taps* the wedge into the flesh of the wood until it's in far enough to stand on its own. It occurs to Lucy that Adam has never split a log before. He grew up in New York City, after all, with parents in academia, and she can't imagine that they'd teach their son such a thing. He lifts the sledgehammer, props it on his right shoulder, and lets it fall onto the wedge. It makes a high-pitched, delicate *ping* sound. He does this again and again. *Ping. Ping. Ping.* The wedge doesn't progress any farther into the wood. Adam glances over his shoulder toward the house.

Busted, Lucy thinks, though she's not sure he can see her. She stares down into the sink full of dishes and waits a moment before she looks up, this time keeping her head tilted down. Adam raises the sledgehammer again, higher this time, way up over his head, and Lucy holds her breath as he swings it down hard, using muscle to add momentum to gravity. There's a loud metal-hitting-metal sound, but the hammer lands slightly in front of its target, clipping the outer lip of the wedge instead of striking it dead on. The wedge shoots back and hits Adam squarely in the shin.

Adam yelps in pain and Lucy runs outside.

"Fuck!" Adam shouts, hopping on his right leg, holding his

left in both hands. "Fuck, fuck, fuck."

Lucy supports him under one shoulder and helps him hobble back inside.

"Fuck."

She sits him down on the futon, takes off his boot, and rolls up his pant leg to unveil an ugly, purple lump the size of a large egg. She runs outside and pats some snow into a disk shape, which she covers in a towel and applies to his injury.

"Fuck."

"What can I do, Adam?"

His look tells her she's done enough already.

"Adam?"

He can't even speak to her yet, he's too angry from the pain, and she can tell that he blames her for his bruised shin—for the whole miserable trip.

"I want to leave," Adam finally says. "I don't want to discuss it. I don't want to feel bad about it. I've just had enough and I want to go home."

While Adam tends his wound in front of the fire, Lucy packs and cleans: She finishes the dishes, unhooks and drains the hose, locks the outhouse, and throws their clothes into bags, which she lugs out to the car and tosses in the backseat. She hops into the driver's seat and turns the key, but the engine won't start. She gets out and looks around: the trunk is ajar.

Back in the house, Adam is anesthetizing himself with the last of the wine and looks content with his notebook opened on his lap, absorbed with an equation.

Lucy's mouth tastes sour. "The battery's dead," she says. "The trunk was open."

Both of them know who left it that way.

"I'm going to walk to the nearest neighbor and see if they can give us a jump," Lucy says.

To his credit, Adam is waiting outside when Lucy returns. She's in the passenger seat of a rusted-out Chevy pickup truck, driven by a man who looks to be in his seventies, wearing a baseball cap and a smile that reveals a gleaming set of dentures.

The man whistles slightly when he speaks. "Only too happy to help a friend of the Wolfs," he says, enjoying the opportunity to rescue city folk. Grabbing the jumper cables from behind his seat, he instructs Lucy to get into the rental car. "Pop the hood for us and when your husband gives you the signal, start the engine. You'll want to give it a little gas, but not too much."

I know how to jump-start a car, Lucy thinks. And he's not my husband! She's suddenly flooded with relief that she and Adam are not married. She gets out of the pickup and, without meeting Adam's gaze, sits in the driver's seat of the rental car.

The old man pops his hood and greets Adam with a neighborly, "Hello." He attaches one end of the cable to his truck's battery and hands the other to Adam, who holds a clamp in each hand and looks bewildered.

Misunderstanding Adam's confusion for marital distress, the old man pats him on the back. "She a little t'ed off about this, eh? Don't worry, we'll have it fixed in a jiffy." He gets back into the truck. "Okay," he calls out. "Hook her up and tell me when!"

From the driver's seat of the car, Lucy watches Adam through the gap between the two raised hoods. He's staring blankly at the engine, clearly not knowing how to attach the clamps. Right out of the Boy Scout manual, my ass! she thinks, furious at Cooper now, too, with all his Yankee-girls-need-to-let-men-be-men crap.

Under normal circumstances, Lucy would try to figure out a way to help Adam without letting him know that she's helping him. But these circumstances are far from normal. She gets out of the car, snatches the jumper cables from him, and tells him to get behind the wheel. Then she clamps the red end to the positive terminal of the battery and the black end to the engine block, and says, "Okay. Now!" to signal the men to start the cars. Adam revs the engine. A few minutes later, she removes the cables in reverse order, looping them around her elbow and wrist, and returns them to the Wolfs' neighbor in a neat coil.

They are halfway home before Adam speaks. "I'm sorry, Lucy. There's nothing I hate more than disappointing you."

Lucy says nothing.

It's a long ride back to the city.

CHAPTER 4

"The male is a domestic animal which, if treated with firmness, can be trained to do most things."

Jilly Cooper

MONDAY NIGHT—KURT BECKER

Martha's FirstDate client Kurt Becker waits for her at the bar of Mare, a celebrity-chef-owned restaurant that's been getting a lot of buzz. When she arrives, only ten minutes late, he greets her with a firm handshake and plenty of eye contact. "It's nice to meet you, Ms. McKenna," he says stiffly. "How do you do?"

"I'm *terrific*," she says. "Call me Martha." Following his greeting, she wonders if hers seems too exuberant, but she's just come from a voice-over audition that turned into a job on the spot, the first acting gig she's had in weeks.

"A voice-over?" Kurt says with uncertainty.

"Voice-overs are to actors what mole removals are to dermatologists. Not glamorous, but necessary. They pay the bills." Lowering her voice, she adds, "The truth is, I'm not the pickiest thespian," and laughs at the thought of how many times that afternoon she'd been made to repeat the line, *It takes grease out of your way,* under the grave direction of an ad exec who advised her to sound more grateful to the product.

Kurt seems taken aback by Martha's gusto, as if it's at odds with the earnest mood he's trying to establish. He laughs awkwardly, and Martha decides to follow his lead and tone down her enthusiasm. He hands her a small, yellow-pink rose, the stem of which is wrapped in a moist paper towel and covered in aluminum foil. "I grew it in my hothouse," he says and attributes his green thumb to his family's Norwegian-bachelor-farmer roots. "I'm experimenting with heirloom roses."

Kurt looks to be in his early forties and Martha finds him unnervingly handsome, with dark blond hair, cool gray eyes, and gleaming, white teeth. She lifts the flower to her nose and for a moment forgets Kurt is not a real date and hasn't grown the rose with the real Martha in mind. She closes her eyes and gets lost in the delicate fragrance of the flowers.

Kurt clears his throat. "You still with me, Martha? Or am I talking to myself here?"

Martha's eyes pop open. *You're on a job,* she reminds herself, *and your client wants his money's worth of your attention.* "Sorry," she says, noticing that when Kurt's handsome face isn't smiling, there's something hard about his mouth and a vein in his forehead promises to bulge when he becomes angry. He has style—always tough to detect in conventional business attire, but discernible to Martha, who's attentive to the subtle wit of tie selection, the play of checks on stripes, the daring vocabulary of collars. She starts to wonder why he hired her—he seems to be a fairly capable dater—and launches into her rote FirstDate questions: "What do you hope to get from this experience?" "How did you hear about FirstDate?" "What do you believe are your dating issues?"

Unlike most of her clients, Kurt is ready with answers. "At the risk of sounding arrogant," he starts right in, "I think I'm a decent catch." He ticks off his attributes one finger at a time until his palms are open, all ten fingers extended: "I'm intelligent, healthy, financially secure, *well* educated, *well* traveled, *well* read—"

Well, well, well, Martha thinks, assuming he's joking.

"—a fine cook, sophisticated, in excellent shape, and shall we say, not horrendously unattractive."

He's not joking.

"Basically," he continues, "I can offer the right woman a pretty good life." His pretty good life includes a house in the country, a fifty-foot schooner, a four-story brownstone on Gramercy Park, and his own plane. "I don't think it's unreasonable that I expect the woman I end up with to have a lot to offer, too." His look asks a rhetorical, *Do you?*

Martha's look doesn't have an answer. But she does find it odd, even if Kurt's fine qualities don't include her personal favorites—warmth and humor—that he hasn't landed someone who likes what he offers enough to stick around. She wonders if he might not be one of those men who wants a woman's love, only to become contemptuous when he gets it; one of the if-you-love-me-then-something-must-be-wrong-with-you types. Kurt's face doesn't look so handsome anymore.

Then his list begins: "The right woman must be intelligent, beautiful, athletic, and a lover of the arts." He goes on to say that money isn't a requirement per se, but an impressive academic record and some level of career success are. "Above all, she can't require a lot of coddling. I need a woman who can hold her own at a business dinner." He pauses and gives Martha a guilty look, perhaps realizing he sounds emotionless. "I'm a real sucker for sad eyes."

Sad eyes? Aren't they usually part of a larger, sad person? Martha wonders.

Mental note: Lose the list.

"Mostly, the woman I'm with needs to understand the pressure I'm under," Kurt says with an urgency that suggests he needs Martha to understand. "I work in a *war zone.* People are being obliterated out there. They're dead before they know what's hit them. That's what it's like in my business every day." He takes a sip of his drink, a double scotch on the rocks. "When I get home, the last thing I need is someone desperate to rehash my day. I need peace."

Martha can't believe that she's blanked on such a major piece of information in his bio. She wishes she could light up a cigarette. "What is it you do again, Kurt?" she asks in her mother's calmest, flight-attendant voice. *Trauma surgeon? Al Qaeda–cell infiltrator? Mob informant?* She can't recall.

"I run a software company," he answers.

Martha quells the urge to laugh and reaches for her napkin.

"Do you have any idea what's been happening in the software industry in the last few years?" he asks incredulously. "It's been decimated. We're dodging bullets."

"Uh-huh." Martha leans back in her chair.

Kurt takes a breath, relaxes his shoulders, and smiles. He turns handsome again. He takes her in, not in a lewd way, but in the way that a man does when he's letting a woman know he finds her attractive. "Enough about my work," he says, allowing his voice to become softer. "Let's get down to romantic business."

Encouraged that he's trying to lighten the mood, Martha smiles back.

"The right woman for me is slender, above five-five, and

under thirty-five . . ." He pauses for a moment as if to gauge if he's unintentionally insulted his date. ". . . so she isn't in too much of a rush to get married and have children."

"Do you feel pressure to get married?" Martha asks.

Kurt adjusts himself in his chair. "Are you always so direct?"

"Pretty much," she answers, though if it were a real date, she knows she'd never have asked the question.

"My motto with women is to take it one day at a time."

That's the Alcoholics Anonymous slogan, too, thinks Martha. "How about we forget about who you want to date and focus on your skills as a dater," she suggests.

Kurt's forehead vein swells a little. "I was only informing you of my minimum standards. I know you're not a matchmaker. You're a dating *expert.*" His emphasis on the word *expert* somehow makes it mean the opposite. "It's not as if I don't know how to treat women."

I didn't hire me, thinks Martha, you did! But still, she wishes she hadn't made Kurt feel defensive. He brings to mind her first foray into psychoanalysis when she was twenty-four. Her goal then was to be declared problem- and neurosis-free, to be told by her shrink that she was wonderfully sane, amusing, talented, and well adjusted. She realizes that's how Kurt is approaching FirstDate, with the goal of being declared a perfect date.

"How about we just try to figure out some new romantic approaches for you?" she says and tries to come up with an appropriate war metaphor that will bring him around, but all that comes to mind is, *Damn the torpedos! Full speed ahead,* which seems more like advice for herself. She opts for a sports cliché instead: "Kurt, we're on the same team here."

It turns out that Kurt speaks Sports as well as War. "All's forgiven," he says, smiling. "Ready for dinner?"

Forgiven? thinks Martha, slightly rankled.

Kurt signals the tuxedoed maître d' and they're escorted from the bar to a lovely table, secluded in a corner. Kurt gently pulls the chair out for Martha. "Just because this isn't a real date doesn't mean that I shouldn't make you feel just as special as I would any woman."

Martha wonders if he's aware of exactly how unspecial saying that would make *any* woman feel.

A waiter rushes over and places a dozen long-stemmed yellow roses on the table, another brings a bottle of Veuve Clicquot, and yet another sets up a bucket of ice. "The world has been very kind to me," Kurt says, elaborating on his trust fund, his Nantucket home, his racing schooner.

When menus don't arrive after twenty minutes, Kurt is compelled to explain that he's taken the liberty of ordering them both the chef's carte du jour.

Mental note: Even if your compulsive list-making has successfully weeded out 95 percent of the female population, you never, ever presume to order for a woman on a first date.

Over their six-course meal, Kurt tells stories in which he quotes people quoting him, makes elaborate displays of wine-tasting, and sends back his filet mignon for being overcooked to medium. "When you spend this much on a meal, you expect perfection," he explains smugly.

And throughout all of it, Martha does what Martha does best: She watches. She studies her date's behavior and tries to enjoy herself. After dessert, she excuses herself, goes to the bathroom, and scribbles notes in a tiny notebook: *Don't brag about being rich, just spare no expense at dinner. Don't boast about your fitness, let me admire your physique. Don't list your academic credentials, dazzle me with your wit.* She looks at herself in the bathroom mirror, noting that she's over thirty-five, has happy eyes, and might even be good for a man like Kurt. She opens her notebook again. *Your list of requirements for a mate is a recipe for staying single: it rules people out. A better way to find the right woman is to be open to her, whoever she is.*

TUESDAY NIGHT—CHARLES FRINGER

Charles leaves a message on Martha's voice mail canceling their dinner date just a few hours before they're supposed to meet. He tells her machine that his weekly meeting has been switched to Tuesdays and he never misses them. Can they reschedule?

Weekly meeting? What could it be? Martha wonders. His parole officer? Anger management? Dinner with mom? Group therapy?

WEDNESDAY NIGHT—WALTER SHERMAN

Martha is her usual ten minutes late, but Walter Sherman arrives even later, pecking away at the buttons on his Blackberry. When he finally looks up, he's unable to find his date among all the leggy starlets who hang out at Bellisima, the Soho hot spot where he suggested they meet. Models and models-in-the-making lean against columns and drape themselves over the stools, crossing and uncrossing their long legs, wrapping and unwrapping their willowy arms around their slender selves. Walter's eyes move from one woman to the next, lingering over their lithe bodies, until at last they land on someone who is actually looking back at him.

Martha? he mouths.

She nods, *yes.* Despite being dwarfed by two statuesque beauties, Martha holds her own at the bar in a red silk blouse, black skirt, and sleek black boots.

He raises an apologetic, just-one-more-minute finger and continues punching buttons.

Martha orders a Chardonnay, which arrives in a thimble-size glass. She downs it in two swallows.

At thirty-four, Walter has not quite grown into his body and the words *overgrown puppy* pop into Martha's head. He has a jowly, droopy face, big ears, and rounded shoulders that hunch over a soft middle. He pads over to Martha, still clutching his Blackberry like a favorite chew toy, and apologizes, offering his free hand to her, his left, and they endure one of those hand-holdy greetings usually reserved for the aged. Martha releases first.

"It was a work thing," he says, placing the device in his pocket and nodding as if they both understand that he had no choice. "I think I might have mentioned that I'm a producer for the *NBC Nightly News*," he says anchorman-style, catching his reflection in the mirror behind the bar and smiling. "The news doesn't stop just because I'm having a drink with a pretty girl."

His Blackberry makes a delayed *ding-dong,* powering-off sound and it occurs to Martha that he might have been playing a game.

"I guess everyone knows how crazy the news business is," he says.

Martha has never been in a newsroom and braces herself for a Kurt-style onslaught of war metaphors.

"Essentially, as the producer, I'm the critical link between world events and you, the TV viewer. I get the news out," Walter says, glancing down the bar. He smiles at the model beside Martha, assuming she might also be listening and, consequently, impressed. "The tricky part is to avoid getting sidelined by all the fame and power. I have to remain clearheaded and objective at all times whether I'm talking to the secretary of state or

Miss America." He interlaces his fingers except for his pointers, which he aims at Martha. "You should check out my Web site: www.walterpsherman.com. It's got some great stuff: Walter's World, Walter's News, Walter's Contact Info." He glances to see if the model is taking notice. She's not.

Mental note: Delusions of grandeur.

"Will do," Martha promises, wondering if Walter has *ever* had a second date.

His beeper sounds and Walter fumbles to remove it from his belt. "Excuse me," he says, bringing the device up close to his face, where he studies its tiny screen and gravely reports seventeen missing in a plane crash in Montana, all presumed dead. He pauses for a moment, then adjusts the beeper to vibrate mode and snaps it smartly back into place on his belt. "Isn't this a great spot?" he says, looking around, whistling as he exhales. "You've got to love how amazingly beautiful and stylish New York women are. I mean, there are more gorgeous women on one block in Soho than there are in the whole state of Kansas."

Mental note: Never assume your date will enjoy admiring women as much as you do.

"Are you from Kansas?" Martha asks, but Walter's distracted by their teen-model waitress, braless in a peasant blouse, who takes them to their table, a linen-covered square crammed along the back wall less than six inches from the next table.

"My name's Ashley," the girl calls out over the rhythmic beat of some too-loud electronica. "What can I get you?" She takes their drink order and bends over to hand them menus, providing an unobstructed view down her blouse. "Let me know if you need anything else!"

"Will do, Ashley. Thanks," says Walter. "Martha, would you mind switching seats? I prefer to observe the crowd. It's how I stay sharp."

Martha feels animosity welling up inside and reminds herself to be professional. *This is not a date, it's a job, and you've been hired to help.* She switches seats and watches Walter check out the happenings at Bellisima. His nose twitches. "What made you decide to try FirstDate?" she asks.

Walter smiles sheepishly. "Would you believe that *two* ex-girlfriends of mine saw your ad and called me?" He laughs. "They both said I was a horrendous first date. Obviously, they were in cahoots and it was some kind of joke, but I thought, Why not? I can use feedback as much as the next guy."

"That's very open-minded," Martha says.

Ashley returns with their drinks: another thimble of Chardonnay for Martha and a seltzer with Rose's lime juice for Walter.

"I like to be alert," Walter says, gesturing to his nonalcoholic beverage.

"Very Bruce Wayne of you," Martha says, picturing a cape and tights in her date's briefcase.

"That's a good one," says Walter, grinning. "If I recall, Clark Kent was in the news business like me, wasn't he? I can't remember what Bruce Wayne did for work."

"Not much, I think," Martha says.

His beeper vibrates again and Walter pounces on it, the small screen glowing with secret information.

"I'm afraid I have to respond to this, Batgirl," he says. "It'll just take a sec." He goes in search of his Blackberry and in the process pulls out a cell phone, a minirecorder, and a GameBoy. When he finds the Blackberry, he thumbs out an e-mail and smiles as he hits *send.* "I think the world is safe again."

Mental note: Stow the toys.

"Now, where were we?" he asks. "Ah. The newsroom . . ."

THURSDAY NIGHT—BOB MCCAB

"Do you like to test your limits?" These are Bob's first words to Martha on the street outside Summit, which turns out not to be a restaurant, but a rock-climbing gym. "Why I warned you to dress casually," he explains, standing beside his motorcycle, wearing old work boots, Levi's, and a leather jacket.

Martha wonders if he's trying to retrieve his youth or if he's never grown up. He's not great-looking, but he's sexy with mussed hair, full lips, and a nose that has been broken at least once.

"I think doing something is the only *real* way to get to know someone," he tells her. "Otherwise, it's all just meaningless patter over lattes, right?"

Martha suspects that Bob has trouble getting *real.* She's discovered that FirstDates are no different than regular dates in that people tend to reveal their issues within the first ten minutes—the trick is to pay attention. The beauty of FirstDate is that Martha doesn't have to ignore these revelations in order to keep romantic hope alive. In fact, it's her job not to.

She follows Bob into Summit and gazes up at the twenty-four-foot-high, pinkish-gray wall, full of crags and dimples, stretching the length of the building. In places, the wall folds back on itself, creating overhangs and cliffs so that thrill-seekers can cling upside down for their full twenty-five bucks' worth of near-death adrenaline.

A Summit teacher hands them harnesses and recites a two-minute lecture on the rules.

"What do you think?" Bob asks.

"Great," Martha says, though she feels the opposite.

"I love your attitude!" Bob helps her on with the gear, securing it across her backside with a pat on her butt. "Now, the most important thing is to be one with the wall," he says in an authoritative voice. With his feet turned out duck-style, he demonstrates how to find footings and holds, and scrambles up a few feet without safety gear. A Summit "ranger" orders him down. Bob's look says, *Get a life.*

"Remember, don't look down," he tells Martha. "Ready?"

"I guess."

As if sensing her trepidation, he starts to encourage her. "This is going to be great!" he says. "You can do it!" And, "Go for the gusto!"

Mental note: Avoid clichés and quoting beer ads.

Martha wonders if this pep talk is for her or for him. Or if he just likes the sound of his own voice.

Then Bob mentions that his ex-girlfriend, Beth, wasn't a risk-taker and that led to their breakup. "My philosophy is to seize the day. *Carpe diem* and all that!"

As she approaches the wall, Martha remembers the rest of that saying: *Carpe diem . . . quam minimum credula postero.* "Put no trust in tomorrow." That's reassuring, she thinks, reaching for the lowest grips, her heart racing. She tries to calm herself by taking a few deep breaths. Why did she just sign a paper relieving Summit of any responsibility for accidental injury or death?

When she's almost twenty feet up, feeling for the grips with her eyes closed, it occurs to her that at thirty-seven, she shouldn't have to do anything she doesn't want to do on a date, let alone be suspended in a harness answering get-to-know-you questions. "I've had enough," she calls down and releases her grip on the wall, trusting Bob not to let her fall.

"Awesome!" he says. "The first time is always the scariest."

Martha says a silent Hail Mary and unfastens her rig. "That was actually my last time."

Bob turns his palms upward. "Teachers only open doors, students must enter alone."

Whatever, Martha thinks, deciding to break her own rule and take charge of the date. "How about some meaningless patter over lattes?"

"That'd be cool, I guess." He suggests a French café around the corner that has wonderful crêpes and coffee. On the walk over, he tells her he is a screenwriter and some of his best work has been done at this café. "Beth thinks the service is slow, but I like that it's so authentically French."

Mental note: Don't talk so much about your ex-girlfriend.

The café is slightly dingy, more like someone's living room than a restaurant, and the two surly waiters don't seem happy to have guests. She and Bob sit in the corner on a frayed love seat where Martha squints to read the blackboard menu on the opposite wall. She orders a cappuccino and a *crêpe fromage* and Bob asks for "the usual," black coffee.

"You're not eating?"

"You know what Hemingway said of Cézanne's pears?" Bob asks. "That they're more beautiful on an empty stomach." He's quiet for a moment. "That's how I want to live my life—appreciating the beauty around me. If it means skipping a meal or two to make the next taste better, so what? Of course, Beth thinks it's because I'm cheap, but she just doesn't get it."

"Exactly how recent is your breakup?" Martha asks.

Bob leans back in his chair and puts his hands behind his head. "If I were to be cynical, I'd say, 'Which one?' The truth is, we've been together on and off for ten years, but our most recent breakup seems more permanent. Beth's changed since her promotion. Suddenly, she wants all this bourgeois crap: a two-bedroom apartment, a summer rental, security, blah, blah, blah. And she wants me to give up my dreams and go corporate, too. We just don't fit anymore, like a donkey's lips don't fit onto a horse's mouth."

Martha cocks her head.

"Ancient Chinese expression."

The waitress puts their coffees on the table with a bored, "Voilà."

"Simply put, we're too different. I like to live large," he continues, opening his arms expansively. "When I die I want my friends to think, 'Now there's a guy who knew how to live.' "

Martha smiles behind the foam of her cappuccino.

"Anyway, I need to get back in the dating circuit, that's all there is to it," he says. "Beth says no woman will want a thirty-eight-year-old man with no prospects, but I say not all women are so superficial. Besides, I'll have the last laugh when my movie's made."

"Don't you think it might be a good idea to wait a little between relationships?" Martha asks, recalling her own experiences in the rebound department.

"Naw, I'm ready," Bob says, pulling a thread on the sofa. "I need someone new, someone with positive energy."

FRIDAY NIGHT—HANNIBAL

Martha is happy to stay at home with Hannibal on Valentine's Day. It's never been a favorite holiday of hers. Her best Valentine's Day ever was spent with Lucy at Madison Square Garden watching the Westminster Dog Show, where they drank cheap champagne served in plastic heart-shaped glasses and remarked on the phenomenon of the tinier the dog, the bigger the walker. Her worst Valentine's Days have been spent in red dresses with men she wished she loved.

This year she rents *Shop Around the Corner,* gives herself a pedicure, orders in sushi (which she shares with Hannibal), and hopes Lucy's romantic weekend is going well.

SATURDAY NIGHT—ALLEN SANDERS

Allen is young and vulnerable and nervous, and Martha has never wanted to help a client more. His face is sweet, lean, and freckled with bashful brown eyes, and he has the kind of curly blond hair you find on little boys at the beach.

"Is this place okay?" he asks.

They're sitting across from each other on high stools at a round table in a lively microbrewery in the Flatiron District.

"It's perfect," says Martha, happy after her rock-climbing date just to be in a restaurant. She looks at the beer menu. "What sounds better to you: Bavarian Weizen or Oatmeal Stout?"

"You're sure you wouldn't prefer Thai or sushi? Maybe a steak house?" Allen asks. "I made reservations at three other places."

"Honestly, this is great. I'm totally happy." Martha orders a stout and eases into her FirstDate questions when their beers arrive. "What would you say is your main dating issue?" she asks.

"Confidence," he says, his hands in constant fluttery motion. "My mom says I came out of the womb shy."

Mental note: Avoid mention of your mother's womb at all costs.

"How do you typically feel when you are on a date?" Martha continues.

Allen thinks for a moment, trying to quiet his hands by placing them on the table, one on top of the other. "Nervous," he says. "Always sure that my date would prefer to be doing something else, with someone else."

Martha can relate to confidence problems, having navigated much of her dating life in character, imitating women she imagined men would want to date. During her teen years, she rotated from one Charlie's Angel to the next, knowing every boy had at least one poster of them over his bed. In her twenties, she tried everyone from Madonna to Cindy Crawford to Julia Roberts. Now, her fallbacks include Miranda from *Sex and the City* and Catherine Zeta-Jones. If a date goes poorly, being in character somehow makes her feel as if someone else has been rejected.

Martha looks across the table at sweet Allen; she hitches up her skirt and crosses her legs. Tonight, she feels a bit like Mrs. Robinson.

Their beers arrive in tall, frosted steins and Allen's long fingers drum the table.

"Tell me what it's like to be a chef," she says, knowing she's helping him along more than she should.

"Well, I still have one semester to go, but I love it," Allen says, visibly relaxing as he describes what it's like to roll pastry, whisk sauces, knead bread. Using his hands as spatulas, he demonstrates how he made a chocolate mousse that afternoon, folding imaginary egg whites into a dense chocolate sauce. "It was sublime," he says, closing his eyes. His hands circle and fold and circle and fold, until the tips of his fingers collide with the rim of Martha's glass, and the beer stein teeters precariously before tumbling toward her.

"Yikes," Martha yelps as it splashes down her front and onto her skirt.

Allen leaps up. "Oh my God, I'm so sorry." He uses his napkin to sop up the beer with awkward pats to Martha's lap. "I'm so, so sorry!"

"Don't worry," Martha says, drenched. "It's just a little beer."

A waitress rushes over with extra napkins, and a busboy toting a mop takes care of the rest. Martha excuses herself to the bathroom to clean up. When she returns, two new glasses of beer are on the table.

Allen looks traumatized. "It's okay if you want to go home. I'll understand."

"What? Over a little spilled beer?" Martha's look says, *Don't be ridiculous.* If Allen were another client, a more resilient one, she might have taken him up on his offer, but she doubts that Allan would reschedule and she really thinks she can help him. "I'm fine, really," she says, pulling her blouse away from her chest where it clings to a lacy bra.

"I just don't know how I could have done anything so stupid. All I did was this—" he says, repeating the folding gesture he'd made moments earlier. What follows is as inevitable as the next wave on the beach: for one slow-motion second, Martha's glass is suspended on its edge, like a basketball player defying gravity under the hoop, and then the laws of physics take hold.

MONDAY NIGHT—BRYCE CARROLL

Martha's on time when she walks through the doors of Bubbly, the champagne lounge that Bryce picked for their date, and sees a neatly dressed man waiting at the bar, facing the door.

He seems to know it's her immediately. "Martha?" he says. "*You're* Martha?"

"That's me," she answers. "You must be Bryce."

He cheek-cheek kisses her, European-style. "I wasn't expecting such a bombshell."

Martha wasn't expecting such unbridled enthusiasm. She feels slightly suspicious.

"You've got this great Andie McDowell thing going on," he says, "but you must hear that all the time." Bryce steps back to take all of Martha in. "Damn! Look at those curls!"

Martha wonders why she's more dubious of a man who compliments her than of one who checks out other women in her presence. She touches her hair, suddenly self-conscious.

"Nice," Bryce says, stroking the soft sleeve of the sweater Martha bought that afternoon. "Prada?"

"How'd you know?"

"I know my designers and I love a woman who can put an outfit together. Now, what can I get you to drink?"

Martha lifts her shoulders and says: "When in Bubbly . . ."

"Perfect." He orders her a glass of champagne and himself a Ketel One martini, straight up, very dry, with a twist. When their drinks arrive, Bryce's martini is "bruised," and he patiently instructs the bartender on the merits of stirring over shaking. "What can I tell you?" he says to Martha. "I'm particular."

Bryce is particular. He wears Diesel jeans, a perfectly pressed oxford shirt, and Gucci tasseled loafers. He tells her he's in advertising and Martha wonders if he gets lots of freebies from clients. It would explain his dewy skin and shiny hair, but before she has a chance to ask, Bryce suggests they trade their best grooming tips.

"PureSkin," he says, touching his face. "Ten percent fruit acid, CoQ10, and lots of vitamin E. Gets rid of spots, fine lines, and makes your skin smoother than you ever thought possible."

Martha's riveted. It's like having a conversation with a girlfriend.

"Your turn," Bryce says. "I have to know what you use on your hair."

"Are you straight?" Martha asks, looking directly into his eyes.

"As an arrow," he replies.

We've just landed on your dating issue, she thinks.

CHAPTER 5

"Women love us for our defects. If we have enough of them, they will forgive us anything."

Oscar Wilde

IN THEIR ENTIRE FRIENDSHIP Martha has never arrived anywhere before Lucy. Yet, there she is, elbows resting on La Luna's shiny bar when Lucy walks in a few minutes late.

Martha looks at the clock. "Where have you been?" she jokes, putting on a worried voice. A glass of Chardonnay sweats on the counter in front of her. "Why haven't you returned my calls?"

Lucy has been hoping to avoid the topic of her unhappy weekend with Adam. "Sorry, I've been completely swamped at work."

"I was here five minutes early," Martha says proudly. "All part of keeping up with my New Year's resolutions."

As Lucy takes off her coat and puts down her shoulder bag, heavy with journals and magazines, she realizes her friend's punctuality will cut significantly into her reading time.

"Have you even noticed that I used the plural?" Martha asks. "Resolution*s*?"

It takes Lucy a moment to grasp the implication. "You have a date? Mr. February? Who is it?"

"Fred," Martha says coyly, somehow making the single syllable sound exotic.

Has Martha ever mentioned a Fred before? Lucy doesn't think so.

"It's a blind date," Martha says.

"And guess who fixed them up?" Eva asks, appearing out of nowhere, both index fingers pointing toward her own round face.

"You don't say." Lucy orders a glass of red wine and once Eva's out of earshot says, "Have you lost your mind?"

"What? Just because Eva's gay means she doesn't know any straight, single men?"

"*We* don't even know straight, single men and we're constantly on the lookout," Lucy reminds her. "Have you forgotten our Christmas party last year? Six couples, eleven single women and seven gay men?"

Martha shrugs.

"What do you know about Eva's taste in men?"

"Lucy, she's the only person who's come up with anyone, okay? One Thursday night with Eva's friend isn't going to kill me."

"Thursday? That's when Cooper arrives. We're all supposed to have dinner."

"Well, you know I'm not going to miss seeing Cooper," Martha says. "I'll stop by after my date."

In the silence that follows, Lucy removes her barrette, which allows a shiny cascade of hair to fall forward. Martha notices some heads turn their way. Blondes do have more fun, she thinks and wonders why her pretty friend doesn't make the small effort it would take to be totally stunning—a bright lipstick, a fabulous blouse, a real haircut. Always pale, Lucy looks positively washed out tonight.

"Is everything okay, Luce?"

Instead of answering, Lucy says, "Do we even know how Eva knows Fred?"

"He's in her pottery class at the Y."

"Pottery class?" Lucy says, the way anyone else might say, *Strip club?*

"What's wrong with that? I kind of like the idea of a man who's interested in exploring his artistic side. It tells me that he's sensual."

"Plus he makes a mean pinch pot," adds Eva, brandishing a bottle of Shiraz.

Lucy says, "Tell us more about your friend Fred."

Eva doesn't know much more: he's in his early forties, has all his hair, is divorced and—she thinks—employed.

Lucy frowns. "That can't really be all you know."

"He shares the wheel nicely?" The bar is getting crowded and Eva doesn't have time for the third degree. "No good deed goes unpunished," she mutters, rushing off to serve an impatient customer.

"For God's sake, Luce, it's just a date. What's with the inquisition?"

What is *with the inquisition?* Lucy takes a deep breath. The image of Adam, clueless with jumper cables, flashes into her head. "I guess it just amazes me how low we set the bar for men these days. Look at you: you're brilliant and gorgeous and talented and funny. And you're being set up with someone whose only known strong points are that he's divorced and not bald."

"Okay. What's really going on here?" Martha asks.

Lucy crosses her arms on the bar and sinks down, head falling forward. "The truth is I'm upset with Adam and I don't mean to take it out on you or Fred or Eva. Things didn't go so well at the farmhouse. Actually, it was a full-on disaster. We came back two days early."

"Oh, sweetie. I'm so sorry." Martha puts an arm across her friend's shoulder. "Tell me everything."

"Give me a few minutes, okay?" Lucy sits up and tries to regain her composure.

"No problem." Martha looks around; the bar is almost full now. "How about we skip the wine tonight and go for a little liquid armor?" she suggests. "I'm thinking tequila."

Lucy knows she's in the hands of a skilled emotional paramedic. "Sounds perfect."

"Play your cards right and I'll tell you some doozie FirstDate stories."

Eva replaces their wine with two shot glasses, several lime wedges, and a small bowl of salt. "Sauza?"

Martha nods.

The first shot carves a delicious channel of heat down their throats and into their chests.

A short, pudgy man standing on his tiptoes on the periphery of a semicircle of dark-suited men catches Martha's attention. He's leaning in, straining to be a part of the group. "What's his deal?" she asks.

"Easy," Lucy says, popping a handful of wasabi peas into her mouth. "A low-ranking gorilla trying to fit in with the big apes. He can't get what he wants on his own, but if he hangs out with them, there's a chance he'll get their leftover food and females."

They call their game zoomorphism.

"Poor chunky monkey," Martha says, already on the lookout for her next subject. "What about that older guy, the sexy one with the red tie?"

Lucy follows Martha's gaze to an attractive man with graying temples at the center of the semicircle. He's just punctuated a point by slapping the bar so hard that the resultant *clap* silences his group and causes their pudgy friend to take a small leap back. The man laughs smugly.

"Duh. He's the alpha. The noise is to intimidate competitors and scare away predators," Lucy says. "Mr. Red Tie is the giant silverback of their troop."

"Hello, Mr. Kong," Martha says in a sugary Fay Wray voice. She flags Eva for another round. "Ready?" she asks Lucy.

"Ready."

They place a pinch of salt on the trampoline of skin between their thumbs and forefingers and on the count of three, lick it off, take the shot, and bite the lime wedge.

Emboldened, Martha sits up tall, arches an eyebrow, and says, "Find me something more interesting than a primate."

Lucy scans the bar.

"What about her?" Eva suggests, nodding toward a voluptuous redhead standing at a table behind them.

Lucy studies the woman, whose hips are swaying to the beat of the Cuban jazz playing in the background. "The behavior is called 'flagging,' " she tells them. "A doe in heat wags her tail to indicate her interest in breeding with available bucks."

"And apparently every buck in this bar is available," Martha says, "even those with wedding rings." She looks around and sees no one she's even remotely interested in flagging. "I'm never going to have any fawns at this rate."

"Newsflash:" Eva says, pouring a pink drink from a shaker. "It's the twenty-first century. We does don't need bucks to have fawns."

Martha's face falls. She can't bear to think about her biological clock driving her to such drastic measures. "How about finding some creature I can relate to, like a black widow spider or a praying mantis?" she asks Lucy. "Something that devours its mate after sex."

A peacock enters in a black leather coat with a rainbow-striped scarf, stopping just past the door to see who's watching him. He struts the long way around the bar to an empty stool.

"Not in the market for a peahen, I'm afraid," Lucy says, bright-eyed and loose.

"What about those two?" Martha asks, pointing down the bar to a well-tanned, fiftyish man showing photographs of some property to a petite Asian woman. He appears eager for a reaction from her but none is forthcoming.

"Weaverbirds!" Lucy says, in a triumph of intellect over alcohol. "When a male weaverbird spots a female he likes, he suspends himself upside down from the bottom of his nest and flaps his wings until he gets her attention so he can show her his home."

"That's the most adorable thing I've ever heard," Martha says. "I'd move in before he could put out a welcome twig!"

"Well, she doesn't look so easy," Lucy says. The Asian woman brushes aside a long strand of black hair and looks away from the gentleman with the photographs.

"Are you suggesting I'm easy?"

"Not exactly," Lucy says, "but let's face it, you're no weaverbird."

"What does a weaverbird do that I don't do?"

"Well, for starters, lady weavers don't mate until after thoroughly inspecting the gentleman weaver's nest," Lucy says. "If it's not up to par, no nookie."

"Wow. Weaver-girls *are* smart," Martha says. "That's it. From this day forward, I'll never get involved with a man without a passing-grade home."

"That's the tequila talking," says Lucy.

"Oh really? What was Adam's apartment like when you met him?"

Lucy makes a face.

"Sorry. I forgot we're not talking about him yet." Martha orders two more shots of tequila.

As Eva pours the drinks, Martha imagines a human version of a male weaverbird, a man willing to flail his wings to get her attention. "Who am I kidding?" she says to Lucy, looking at the amber liquid and feeling its effects. "I'd always overlook a shoddy nest for someone who tries hard enough to win my love."

"Me, too," Lucy says, clinking Martha's tiny glass. "Adam was *sharing* a studio in Hell's Kitchen when I first met him. Why do you think he moved into my place?" She salts her hand. "We should try to learn something from the female weaver because at least they act with their own reproductive interests in mind."

"To thinking more like weaverbirds," Martha toasts, quickly downing her third shot. "Why aren't we more like them?"

"Humans don't approach mating in a particularly pragmatic way." Lucy thinks of her relationship with Adam and frowns. "Love just isn't a very precise tool for measuring the evolutionary advantages of hooking up with one guy over the next."

Martha can see her friend is headed for a maudlin meltdown. "Want to hear about my FirstDates?" Without waiting for an answer, she launches into her stories, greatly exaggerating each of her client's flaws. She tells Lucy how Kurt punctuated all his sentences with battle sounds, how Walter kept dropping his fork to get the waitress in the billowy blouse to bend over, how Bryce offered to give her a facial using the bar's pre-

prepared garnishes of olives and lemons.

Soon Lucy is laughing so hard tears are streaming down her cheeks.

"At least they were trying!" Martha laughs right along with her.

"It counts for something," Lucy agrees, wishing Adam would try harder. "But here's what I'm curious about. What do you say to them during their follow-up sessions? How do you tell someone like Walter he's got to stop ogling? Or Bryce to lose the gay vibe?"

"Metrosexual vibe," Martha corrects. "It varies from man to man. Take Kurt, for instance. He's a smart guy. At our follow-up meeting, I told him that bragging about a fat bank account actually makes him seem insecure, not the opposite."

"The ole luxury-sports-car-equals-a-small-johnson theory?"

"Exactly. And he got it right away. It's just that . . ." Martha's voice trails off.

"Go on," Lucy prompts.

"FirstDate has a fatal flaw," Martha says. "One date just isn't enough. How can I hope to help these men in two or three hours? They've spent twenty or thirty years becoming who they are. It's not enough to tell them not to talk on their cell phone or to chew with their mouths closed."

Lucy nods.

"These guys don't just need pointers on how to get a second date," Martha continues. "They need lessons on how to be successful in full-fledged relationships."

"Like what?"

"I don't know . . . general how-to-be-better-men sorts of lessons," Martha says, biting into a lime wedge. "Classes in everything from confidence to carpentry to chivalry. And those are just the *C*'s."

"Well, have I ever got a *D* for you, baby," Lucy says, describing Adam's total lack of skill behind the wheel. She pitches herself forward and back to illustrate what the trip was like, unintentionally slipping off the her bar stool in the throes of her demonstration.

"You okay?" Martha holds Lucy's arm as she climbs back on.

"Every man should know how to drive well," Lucy continues in a slightly drunken yet professorial voice, as if nothing had happened.

"Here, here," Eva chimes in. "Men need lessons on just about everything: how to order wine, make a bed, dance, build a fire—"

"An absolute must!" Lucy interrupts. "In fact, they should be required to master all the basic caveman skills: how to kill small animals, scare away big ones, find water. All that stuff."

"And the modern caveman should know how to change a tire," Martha adds, picturing her brother stranded on the side of the road.

"Not to mention how to jump-start a car," Lucy says, opening the floodgates and letting the whole disappointing story of her weekend with Adam pour out: the eagle comment, the outhouse debacle, the wood-chopping fiasco, every cringe-worthy moment. "It went beyond ineptitude," she tells them. "It was as if Adam was letting me know that he wasn't up to the task of being my mate, like he was saying, 'These are my limitations. Look at me, I can barely provide for myself. I'm not ready to be a husband or a father.' "

"I don't think that's what he meant to convey," Martha says. "I know he's screwing up right now, but try to remember how much he loves you."

Lucy blows her nose in a damp cocktail napkin. "Not easy to do when he's acting like such a total idiot. The man consoles himself with *math*. He's completely absent. It's like I'm the administrative assistant for our relationship: I have to do everything from arranging our vacations and planning dinners to envisioning our future."

At a loss for words, Martha pulls Lucy toward her and gives her forehead a quick kiss.

"What's happened to men?" Lucy asks, slurring slightly. She rolls a dried wasabi pea underneath her index finger. "Were our fathers like this and we just didn't notice? Or did feminism somehow interfere with the natural order of things? Maybe men were threatened when women intruded on the sacred male territory of work. Instead of picking up the slack at home, they checked out entirely."

Eva and Martha exchange a wary look, and Eva pours Lucy a large glass of water.

"In the words of Gloria Steinem," Lucy says, getting onto her soapbox, "I have yet to hear a man ask for advice on how to combine marriage and career." She crushes the pea under her thumb, leaving a little green mess.

Eva looks at the pea dust. "How about we don't overintellectualize this. They're men and they've been this way since the dawn of time. Sooner or later, anthropologists will discover that they've been duped by cave drawings for centuries: cavemen were only *fantasizing* when they drew those macho killing-woolly-mammoths scenes on the wall; what they were really doing was killing time, sitting on their fuzzy asses and doing a little sketching while they waited for the women to return with food."

Martha snorts with laughter. "My own theory is that it's a city problem. Don't country men know how to do all those basic manly things?"

"In your dreams," Eva says.

"No, Eva, Martha's got a point," Lucy says. "My friend

Cooper is from the South and he's manly."

"And gentlemanly to boot," Martha adds.

"You'd think city guys would at least make up for their lack of manliness with some extra chivalry, but no."

"So, we'll teach them!" Martha says, lighting up at the thought. "Where did you guys learn how to build a fire?"

"Nauset Girls Camp," Lucy says.

"Camp Mashunga," Eva says.

"That's it!" Martha shouts, slapping her hands on the bar and nearly knocking over the bowl of peas. "It's so obvious. We'll start a camp for men!"

Lucy laughs. "Apparently, I'm not the only one who's had too much to drink."

"We'll call it Man Camp," Martha says.

"That's kind of catchy," Lucy admits. "Okay, I'm in. And Adam will be the first camper."

"Jesse's number two," Martha says. "If that boy's going to have any chance with Andrea, he needs a masculinity booster shot."

"Your FirstDate guys could use the help, too," Eva says, and then lowers her voice. "Not to mention most of my customers."

Tired and tipsy, Lucy announces that it's time for her to go home. She has to teach freshman biology in the morning and already feels tomorrow's hangover looming in the back of her head.

Eva charges them for two shots of tequila, which Lucy insists on paying for. She pulls a twenty-dollar bill out of her wallet, on which Adam has stuck a Post-it note. *I'm thinking about you right now,* it says. She peels it off and tucks it into the outer pocket of her wallet, where a dozen other Post-it love notes are stored: *I love you like thunder. Be mine forever. I wish I had you in my arms.* Usually his messages seem adorable, but tonight they just seem short.

Lucy leaves Eva a gigantic tip and she and Martha stagger outside into the night air, giggling as they wend their way home to the Kingston. They walk arm in arm and point out random men. "Send him to Man Camp," they whisper to each other. They say, "camper," about the man who lets his wife pick up their toy poodle's deposit as he looks away, pretending not be the poodle-dad. They say it about the stooped-over man who, berated by his shrill wife, keeps repeating, "You're right. You're right. I'm sorry." And they say it about the man who enters their building before them, allowing the door to click closed in their faces.

"Man Camp for all of them," Martha says, swiping her magnetic key across the box and holding open the door as Lucy scoots under her arm.

Once inside, Lucy suddenly gets serious. "God, Martha. Can you imagine what we'd think if some guy proposed Woman Camp?" She pictures classes on how to churn butter and darn socks.

"Don't harsh my mellow," Martha says. "We're in the land of make-believe and we can do whatever we want, and I want to round men up and send them off."

"Okay, Tinkerbell."

They hug good night and walk in opposite directions down the long central corridor. Lucy hears Martha sing her own version of "Where Have All the Flowers Gone": "*Where have all the young men gone?/ Gone to Man Camp every one/ That's where they'll finally learn/ That's where they'll finally learn.*"

CHAPTER 6

"Women want mediocre men, and men are working hard to be as mediocre as possible."

Margaret Mead

MARTHA CAN'T DECIDE what to wear for her blind date with Fred. Clothes are strewn all over the Bordello—across the bed, over the backs of armchairs, on the floor. She tries on several variations of her standard FirstDate outfit: a fitted black skirt paired with a colorful blouse and chic, pointy-toed black boots. But tonight no combination feels right and she worries that her work uniform might seem too brisk and businesslike. This is a *real* date, after all.

If only she could come up with the perfect character to play for her evening with Fred, then maybe the perfect outfit would follow. But who'd be right for the job? Marilyn Monroe? Audrey Hepburn? Catherine Deneuve? Somehow, channeling a legendary star seems beyond her ability tonight and she wonders why she can't come up with some garden-variety fabulous woman. Someone irresistible and smart and funny. Someone like Lucy.

That's brilliant, she thinks. I'll go as Lucy Stone. She pours herself a glass of wine and picks up a CD that Lucy recently loaned her, thinking it might help get her in the mood. It was a Christmas gift from Cooper, a compilation of his favorite tunes entitled *Farm Songs.* Martha flips over the CD and studies the photograph of the farm on the cover. There are cows in the foreground and a man in the distance, who Martha guesses might be Cooper. The man's wearing jeans and a checked shirt and has a huge two-man crosscut saw, longer than he is tall, balanced across his sturdy shoulders. He is walking away from the photographer on a dirt road bordered by a fence. Martha wonders if Fred has ever even *seen* a saw like that.

The first song is "Hey, Good Lookin'," and Martha takes this as a positive sign. She turns the volume up and sings, "Whatcha got cookin'?" as she dances down the hallway in a matching lime-green Cosabella bra and thong. Once in the bedroom, she wriggles into a snug pair of low-riding brown cords, slings a wide belt across her hips, and nods approvingly at herself in the mirror. Now, what would Lucy wear on top? she wonders. The last thing Lucy borrowed from her was an ivory angora cardigan, which Martha thinks might do the trick (especially if she leaves it unfastened a button or two below where Lucy would). She puts it on and it's perfect, right down to the tiny triangle of tummy left bare where the sweater opens slightly below the last button.

During Patsy Cline's bittersweet "Sweet Dreams," Martha applies some barely there, Lucy-style makeup, while envisioning the entire, tragic trajectory of her love affair with Fred: their first kiss, a brushstroke of blush; their first fight, a swipe of mascara; infidelity, a dab of lip gloss; abandonment, a dusting of powder. *You don't love me, it's plain,* sings Patsy. *I shoulda known I'll never wear your ring.* Martha puts her hands on either side of the bathroom sink and stares hard at the results. Despite the anguish of imagined heartbreak on her face, the lack of makeup suits her. Her dark eyes glisten and her skin looks dewy.

You should've thought about all this before you dumped me, Fred, Martha thinks, forwarding the CD to a more upbeat song.

LUCY IS IN A SCRAMBLE to get her place ready for Cooper's visit. If his plane landed on time, he'll arrive any minute. Most of the items on her checklist are done: she's put sheets on the sofa bed, cleaned the bathroom, put out new votive candles. All that remains is to cook a perfect dinner, over which she wants Cooper and Adam to get to know each other better. They've met a few times, but always when one or the other was in a rush, so their exchanges have been mostly handshakes in person and how-are-yous over the phone. Though Lucy can't imagine that they won't like each other, she knows that a tasty meal, mellow music, and a great bottle of Cabernet do a lot to further a friendship.

When the phone rings, Lucy assumes it's Cooper calling to tell her that his plane is delayed or his luggage is missing, but she hears Martha's voice on a static-filled cell-phone line.

"What's up, dater?" Lucy asks, chopping onions with the phone cradled between her chin and shoulder, her eyes starting to water.

"Um. Not much," Martha says, hesitating. "I seem to have taken a detour on my way to meet Fred."

Lucy puts down the knife and looks at her watch; it's 7:10 P.M., ten minutes after Martha's date was supposed to start.

"What kind of detour?"

"I'm at an Irish pub across the street from where I'm supposed to meet him."

Lucy hears the tinkle of ice cubes in a glass as Martha takes a sip of something.

"Luce, what's wrong with me?"

"You're just nervous." Lucy rinses her hands and goes to the living room, where she sits down on the floor, her spine against the sofa. "What's going on?"

"I have no idea. But I think the problem is as simple as I'm not you."

Confused, Lucy says, "That seems like a good thing."

"No, you see, as far back as I can remember I've gotten into character for dates." Martha has never told this to anyone. "I usually choose celebrities: Mae West if I'm feeling sassy, Audrey Hepburn if I want to be glamorous. You get the idea. Anyway, tonight I thought it might be fun to be you."

Lucy digests the information, unsure she likes the idea of Martha playing her.

"But it didn't work," Martha continues. "In the cab ride over, the real me kept coming through so loudly I couldn't ignore her."

Relieved, Lucy asks, "Well, uh, what did the real you say?"

"That you wouldn't be caught dead doing something this neurotic."

True, Lucy thinks. "What I don't quite understand is why you're so anxious about a date with a man you've never met. An amateur potter, no less."

Martha is quiet for a moment. "I guess I just don't think I could handle it right now if some Fred Nobody made me feel like I wasn't pretty enough or young enough or witty enough."

Hearing this, Lucy is flooded with gratitude for Adam's

presence in her life. She lifts one of the sofa's cushions in search of a Post-it love note, but finds none. "Martha, if you go as you, that won't happen!"

"You're just saying that because you're my best friend." Martha sighs. "Besides, you have no idea of the person I become on dates; she's nothing like the me you know. You'd hate her."

"I doubt that."

"It's true! I become this pathetic, smiley, unopinionated, über-hostess. I ask questions like: 'How are you finding your soup?' and 'Isn't this place delightful?' I kid you not, I use words like *delightful.* Lucy, it's awful, I become *my mother.*"

"Look," Lucy says, "Here's what I want you to think about tonight." She's not quite sure what to say next. "Think: I'm Martha McKenna: actress, entrepreneur, fabulous woman. You are Fred Nobody, some unknown entity who must prove himself worthy of my company." Lucy pauses a moment. "I've got it: go as a peahen!"

"What?"

"In nature, males are always in charge of courtship and seduction. Remember? Meet Fred with that in mind. Make *him* do the work. Think: Fred is just one of a hundred peacocks who wants to mate with me."

"Okay," Martha says, clearly dubious but willing to grasp at any straw.

Lucy gets up and paces across the living room. "These are the questions you should ask yourself when you're at dinner. Fred, do your tail feathers please me? Do I like your song? Am I into your mating dance or does your chest-puffing just make you look bloated?"

There's no reply.

"You with me?"

"Coo," Martha says in the affirmative. "Coo."

"Atta girl!" Lucy fights an impulse to correct Martha's dove impersonation. "Remember, make *him* do the work!"

"Right. Make *him* do the work. Make *him* do the work. Okay, I better get over there, Luce. I've already made my peacock wait twenty minutes."

FOR DINNER, Lucy serves her favorite Cape Cod dish, linguine with white clam sauce. As a child, at least once a week during the summertime, she and her father would slog through the mud pools in the marshes of Nauset Bay, fending off greenhead flies and no-see-ems to find the delicate clams for this dish. Tonight's clams, however, are from Whole Foods, along with an array of exotic greens. When Lucy is depressed about living in New York, she likes to remind herself that it's one of the few places on earth where you can find baby arugula 24/7, no matter the season. She tosses on some goat cheese, pear slices, and a small handful of crushed walnuts, then puts the bowl into the refrigerator to crisp.

Adam shows up with a bouquet of flowers bought at the corner bodega. "Smells delicious," he calls from the hallway, bolting the door behind him. Lucy's back is to him when he walks into the kitchen and he kisses the nape of her neck, sending a shiver down her spine.

She turns around to kiss him on the mouth. "Flowers! How sweet." She has a clam in each hand and a pile of already scrubbed ones in the sink. "Put them in a vase for me?"

Adam reaches for a vase, then cuts through the bouquet's plastic wrapping. The stems are coated with slime and when he lifts the flowers out, half of the petals stay behind. He looks to see if Lucy's noticed—she hasn't—and quickly arranges the flowers, trying to hide the gaps.

"How was your day, sweetie?" Lucy asks, expecting an animated review of the behavioral economy lecture he was supposed to attend.

Instead, Adam tells her about the ergonomist from Mt. Sinai who came to observe him at work and assess how his computer setup and work habits contribute to his chronic back pain. "You can't imagine how many things I'm doing wrong, Luce: my screen's too far away, I overuse the mouse, my chair's too low."

Lucy wipes her hands on her apron before taking it off. "Did he have any suggestions for what to do?"

"More breaks."

More breaks? Lucy wonders if Adam will finish his dissertation before mandatory retirement.

"He also advised me to buy a tented keyboard and one of those hands-free phones, but they're both kind of expensive." Adam rubs his lower back area. "And that I go to an orthobionics bodywork person for massage."

"Bodywork?" Lucy says skeptically, thinking of the thinly veiled ads for sexual services listed under that heading in the backs of magazines like *New York* and *Time Out.* "Are you in pain right now?"

Adam nods.

"How about a drink?" Lucy suggests, wondering if he remembered to pick up the wine. He hadn't brought any into the kitchen.

"Wine should be here any moment," Adam says, clearly pleased not to have forgotten. "The ergonomist told me that until I'm asymptomatic, I shouldn't lift anything heavy, so I had a half case delivered."

When the doorbell rings a few moments later, it isn't the deliveryman but Cooper, whose six-foot frame fills the door. With a duffle bag slung over his shoulder and a couple bottles of wine in the other, he scoops up Lucy for a bear hug, lifting her feet off the ground.

Adam stands to one side as they embrace, studying Cooper's face over Lucy's shoulder. He's a big man with a great flop of brown hair that falls almost to his eyes and sideburns that slice across well-tanned cheekbones. Adam nods hello and Cooper nods back, handing him the duffle bag, which is heavier than Adam expects and lands on the floor with a thud.

—

There are twelve tables in the restaurant and only one man sitting alone. Fred. He's wearing a bright yellow V-neck sweater over a blue Oxford shirt. Although he's facing the door, he's too busy depilling the arm of his sweater to notice Martha as she enters.

Martha comes to the table and introduces herself.

"Hello," Fred says. "Nice to finally meet you."

Martha slides into the banquette across from him. In between them is a sunken burner, which a slender, kimono-clad waitress comes by to ignite, placing a pot of water above it.

"I'm sorry I'm late," she says.

"Not a problem," Fred says, but Martha can tell that it is. "Before I became a father, I used to be a late person myself." Fred goes on to explain that he's a newly divorced, stay-at-home dad with two young daughters. "Nothing like children to get your priorities straight. They force you to become a better person than you knew you could be."

Martha imagines Lucy's reaction to the news that Fred-the-potter doesn't have a real job. Then she feels guilty. Is it sexist to have reservations about dating a full-time dad? To say nothing of the potential stepchildren Eva never mentioned? The word *homemaker* pops into her head.

The pot of water between them starts to boil.

"Have you had shabu-shabu before?" he asks. "I'm partial to foods that you have to work for: lobster, artichokes, pistachios. I think the effort makes them taste better."

Soon their waitress presents them with a beautiful tray of thinly sliced beef and artfully arranged vegetables. She hands Martha a tool, some hybrid of a ladle and strainer, and shows her how to skim the froth off the top of the boiling liquid.

Martha tries to give Fred the benefit of the doubt. "How does it work as a stay-at-home-dad now that you're divorced?" she asks, using chopsticks to put some bok choy in the bubbling water. Although no scum has developed yet, she skims the top with her special spoon.

"Pretty much the same as it always did," Fred says, "except now I have my own place. I still spend the days at my ex-wife's apartment with the girls." He tosses some other vegetables into the pot and pokes at them. "Want to see pictures?"

Before Martha has a chance to answer, Fred comes around the table and slides in beside her. She scoots over close to the wall and concentrates on skimming the brownish-yellow bubbles off the surface of the broth. Steam is billowing up from the pot and Fred's arm has found its way across the top of the banquet behind her. She feels claustrophobic.

Fred flips through photos of his adorable daughters—at the merry-go-round, in the bath, on the beach. "Aren't they precious?"

"Mm," Martha agrees, putting two slices of beef in the broth and elbowing Fred in the process. "Ready to eat?" She looks at the empty bench across the table.

"Oh, I'm sorry," Fred says, removing his arm but remaining

in her space. "Full disclosure time: you're my first date since my wife and I split up, and I guess I'm a little nervous." He laughs. "Okay, I'm a lot nervous. I even scheduled an emergency session with my shrink this afternoon."

Martha is tempted to advise Fred not to discuss his psychotherapy on a first date but reminds herself he's not a client.

BACK AT THE KINGSTON, Lucy and Cooper and Adam are sitting around the dinner table, twisting succulent forkfuls of linguine into their mouths. The meal is delicious and both men seem to be relaxed and enjoying each other's company, though Adam did squeeze her hand in surprise when Cooper said grace.

But now the wine is flowing, as are Cooper's stories of life on Tuckington Farm, and Lucy and Adam are mesmerized. He tells them about the hardships of the record-cold winter they'd had: the failure of various machines—his tractor, a bailer, the farm's "honey wagon" (a vehicle that spreads manure); how a portion of his herd got an infection of the udders called mastitis that had to be treated with antibiotics, rendering the whole herd's milk unsellable for a time; how a farmhand accidentally ripped open one of two huge, hundred-foot-long silage bags, ruining much of the spring fodder.

"The truth is, it's been the toughest winter since I took over the farm," Cooper says. "Thank God for spring." He takes another bite of pasta and smiles at Lucy appreciatively.

"How's Pinckney?" Lucy asks, referring to Cooper's prize bull.

"Trouble," he says. "Lots and lots of trouble. Darn beast tore clear through the fence last week to go after the neighbor's Holstein. They've been waging war all winter, bellowing at each other like dinosaurs. With the first sign of spring, ole Pinckney decided he needed to suss out the competition."

"What did you do?" Lucy asks, putting down her fork.

"Well, there was nothing to do but watch, really. Neither had horns, thank God, but the battle went on for hours. They rolled each other over, smashed fences, bashed in each other's ribs, even took down a small tin shed." Cooper uses his utensils as surrogate bulls.

"That's unbelievable," Lucy says. "Why can't anything that exciting ever happen around here?" She grabs Adam's hand and suggests they flee the city and buy a farm.

Adam looks at her as if she's crazy. Their Valentine's Day trip was less than two weeks ago.

"Do I need to remind you that my mornings start with shoveling muck at five A.M.?" Cooper asks. "Does that sound exciting to you?"

"Shut your pie hole," Lucy says, an expression she picked up from him in college. "You've got the best life of anyone I know!"

"You're right. Dairy farming is undeniably glamorous. As you know, most of my time is spent fending off the advances of supermodels."

Lucy rolls her eyes.

Cooper looks at Adam over the bedraggled bunch of flowers, suddenly aware that he's dominated the evening's conversation. "I've shot off at the mouth quite enough for one night. Tell me more about what you do, Adam."

Adam shakes his head. "I always find crazed-bull stories a tough act to follow."

"Nonsense," Lucy says, squeezing Adam's forearm. "The world's most influential thinkers are starting to pay attention to behavioral economists."

"Lay it on me," Cooper says enthusiastically. "You don't want me to return to West Virginia unable to impress the supermodels."

Lucy smiles encouragement at Adam. *Go on!*

Adam has no choice. "Essentially, behavioral economy offers an alternative to classic economic theory, which assumes people are rational beings living in a perfectly efficient market." He speaks rapidly, wanting to get the spiel over with. "Behavioral economists concentrate on the *ir*rational things people do, using psychology to explain behaviors like altruism or buying unnecessary items. Our goal is to improve the predictiveness of conventional economic models by plugging them into more realistic formulas for how people actually behave."

Cooper is genuinely interested. "What's your area of expertise?"

"Procrastination," says Adam, looking at his pasta. "Procrastination has huge economic implications."

Having just covered Adam's portion of the rent again, Lucy thinks, I'll say it does.

Adam continues: "For instance, lots of people procrastinate in taking advantage of 401K plans, even though they know they're good for them."

"And what do behavioral economists think should be done about that?"

"Most would probably argue that government should create policies that acknowledge procrastination and make 401K deductions automatic rather than opt-in plans."

"Interesting premise," Cooper says, "although I must admit, I strongly disagree with it."

Adam cocks his head.

"The idea of creating policies to coddle procrastinators seems wrong," Cooper says. "The government should encourage people to be self-sufficient, not accommodate laziness. We don't want a dependent populous."

Adam laughs nervously and is about to launch into a rebuttal when Lucy grabs his knee under the table and squeezes, *You're totally right, but please change the subject.*

Not fluent in Squeeze, Adam feels reprimanded and clams up.

"I want to visit the farm," Lucy blurts out.

Cooper registers the alarm on her face and looks back at Adam. "I'm sorry," he says. "How about we skip politics for now? Lucy'll tell you, I'm just a pigheaded, old conservative. The only way we've managed to stay friends all these years was to agree not to discuss politics."

Adam nods and wonders why Lucy never mentioned that Cooper is a rabid-Fox-TV-watching-Bible-thumping-Second-Amendment-he-man. He's never known one personally before.

IT'S AFTER 10 P.M. when Martha knocks on Lucy's door. "You are the Albert Einstein of dating!" she proclaims, hugging her friend. "The night was a bust, but your advice was awesome!"

Lucy responds with a *shush* and a finger over her lips. "Adam already went to bed. He has to give a lecture first thing tomorrow morning. But come on in. Cooper and I are still working on dessert."

Out of the corner of her eye, Martha sees Cooper rise from the sofa and turns to walk toward him, hips swaying. "Oh, hello, Man-Who-Stands-When-I-Enter," she says.

"Can I get you a glass of wine?" Lucy asks.

"Please," Martha says, flopping down on the sofa opposite where they've been sitting. She kicks off her boots and puts her feet up, stretching her long legs. Her angora sweater pulls up, baring a couple of inches of pale midriff. "So what brings you to our fair city this time?"

"Simply the prospect of drinking wine with the two most fabulous women on earth," Cooper says, momentarily averting his eyes from her belly to open the bottle of wine Lucy has handed him.

"And are there others of his kind, Lucy?"

"Cooper tells me they're all like him in West Virginia," Lucy replies, wanting to toss a throw over Martha's midriff. She pulls down her own sweater, as if to set an example.

"I've never said any such thing," Cooper says, unable to take his eyes off Martha. "I can assure you, I'm one of a kind. Now, what great dating advice did the formidable Ms. Stone give you?"

"Oh, just the usual stuff: wear clean underwear and think like a peahen," Martha says.

"Of course," he says, playing along, bewildered but utterly charmed by Martha.

"Well?" Lucy says impatiently. "How'd the date go?"

"It was perfectly nondescript," Martha says, smiling. "Like the peacock himself. I have no idea what I was so scared of. Fred's tail feathers were beige, his song was off-key, and his idea of a mating dance was to discuss the revelations he's made in therapy since his divorce."

"Sexy," Lucy says with zero enthusiasm. She looks at Cooper. "See? I'm not exaggerating when I tell you about this stuff. This is something we deal with all the time: men who are just a little too in touch with their sensitive side."

Martha chimes in: "And don't forget the metrosexuals."

"Metro-whats?" Cooper asks.

"You know: metrosexuals," Lucy says. "Guys who are straight

but like expensive face creams, wear only custom-tailored shirts, and would never think to order a martini without specifying a chic brand of vodka: Grey Goose or Ketel One."

"That's right," Martha adds. "Men in New York enjoy therapy, yoga, and the Barney's warehouse sale. And they *love* talking about their feelings."

"Good Lord," Cooper says.

"And metrosexuals aren't even the worst of what's out there in the dating pool," Martha tells him.

"This is totally mind-boggling," Cooper says, stuttering with disbelief. "Do you realize that if you two lived in West Virginia, men would be fighting to open doors for you?" He starts to lift his wineglass, but puts it back down to keep talking. "Hell, they'd walk a mile in the rain to get you a ham sandwich, if that's what you wanted."

Lucy and Martha beam. Even though they don't believe a word of it, there's nothing like hearing one of Cooper's how-men-should-treat-women rants.

"Don't these men know how expendable they are?" Cooper asks. "With their pathetic little Y chromosome and all its junky DNA? As I see it, a man's job is to prove himself indispensable or risk becoming, well, dispensable."

"Reproductively speaking, you're totally on the mark," Lucy says, and explains the concept to Martha: "A small number of high-quality males would be a perfectly efficient way to serve the reproductive needs of all women."

Cooper nods. "It only takes one bull to breed all the cows on any farm," he says. Then he looks at Martha longingly. "Though I like to think human men can offer things other than sperm: protection, security, and adoration."

Uncomfortable under Cooper's gaze Martha says, "Well, if tonight has convinced me of anything, it's that I need to focus on FirstDate, on business. Real dating is too discouraging."

DURING THE COURSE of his weeklong visit, without any hinting or prodding, Cooper does every single thing that Lucy and Martha need doing. He stops by Martha's apartment, and with a few swift strokes of a hammer fixes the slanted shelf that Jesse put up. He installs an extra phone jack in Lucy's bedroom, snakes her clogged bathroom sink, and puts together a modular desk so that she can work at home. He holds doors, pulls out chairs, takes the girls to movies, and eloquently discusses everything from wine to politics to dairy farming, all while exuding masculinity and chivalry in a completely unself-conscious way, a way that is wholly unfamiliar to Lucy and Martha in their daily life in New York.

The day before Cooper is to leave, Lucy's new sofa arrives. Her doorman intercoms her when the deliverymen refuse to bring it up to her apartment.

"Their slip says 'curb-to-curb' service," the doorman says, "and they say it'll be an additional two hundred dollars to bring it up."

Lucy is appalled. "To roll it onto an elevator?" But by the time she gets downstairs, the deliverymen have left and the sofa, wrapped in heavy-duty plastic, is sitting out on the curb. "Would you call maintenance for a dolly?" she asks the doorman.

"Of course, Miss Stone," he replies. "Always happy to lend a hand."

"Thanks," she says, relieved to know that chivalry isn't entirely dead.

"You take care of me and I'll take care of you," he says.

Having had every intention of tipping him, Lucy feels indignant that he's suggested it. When the dolly arrives, she tells him she'll manage without him. But how? Adam's in bed, doped up on painkillers from having thrown out his back rearranging his office computer per his ergonomist's instructions, and Cooper is having breakfast with some other college friends. She calls Martha on her cell phone, waking her up even though it's past 11 A.M.

Five minutes later, Martha shows up on the sidewalk looking disheveled.

"Late night?" Lucy asks.

"Kinda." Martha isn't much of a talker before her third coffee.

The sofa is heavy but they attempt to heave half of it on top of the dolly, which keeps skidding away from them across the sidewalk.

They're sitting on the sofa outside, debating their options, when Cooper returns from breakfast. "What on earth?" he asks, gently moving them aside. He shimmies the sofa onto the dolly and deftly maneuvers it up the wheelchair ramp and into the Kingston, where the doorman stands. "What the hell's wrong with you, just standing there like a bump on a log while these ladies struggle?"

The doorman shrugs. "It's not in my job description to haul furniture."

Cooper glares at him. "You weren't exaggerating, were you?" he says to Lucy. "Where the hell is your boyfriend? Who lets a woman move a sofa alone?"

"Hey," Lucy says, feeling protective. "You know Adam threw his back out."

"Ridiculous," Cooper mutters. He shifts the sofa to its side and guides it onto the elevator, sweat beading on his brow.

Martha imagines the muscles on Cooper's back working underneath his sweater. She hooks arms with Lucy. "Finally, a man who doesn't need Man Camp!"

"Sadly, for every one who doesn't, there're about six who do," Lucy says, looking back at the doorman as they board the elevator. "He gets a one-way ticket."

"A Man Camp lifer," Martha agrees.

Cooper looks at them curiously. "What did you just say?"

Lucy and Martha lock eyes. *Busted!* The elevator doors swoosh together.

"Out with it," Cooper says. "What is Man Camp?"

"Can you keep a secret?"

CHAPTER 7

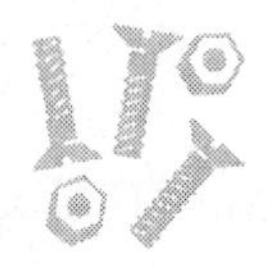

"Nobody will ever win the battle of the sexes. There's too much fraternizing with the enemy."

Henry Kissinger

"REMIND ME AGAIN why we're going to the Guggenheim?" Martha asks, unable to imagine anything less fun to do on Cooper's last day in town. They are headed uptown on a packed Madison Avenue bus, elbows hooked around a metal pole to keep from bumping into other passengers as the vehicle lurches in traffic. "I get motion sick every time I walk down that huge spiral."

"We're going for culture, my dear," Lucy says. "Don't you think it's a little ridiculous that we live here and never go to museums?"

Martha shrugs. She'd been pushing for lunch in the Village or a shopping excursion to Soho.

"Even Cooper managed to make it to the Matisse-Picasso exhibit," Lucy adds.

"Now, that was a great show," Cooper says. "Though, if you ask me, it should've been called: 'Picasso's a Little Better.' "

Martha laughs and repeats the line, nudging Lucy, as if her friend didn't hear it or she'd be laughing, too.

It's not *that* funny, Lucy thinks and takes a few steps toward the window to see what street they're on. Her view is blocked by fluffy parkas and grimy windows, making it hard to read the numbers on the tiny green signs as they whiz by.

All at once the bus bounces to a stop and Martha loses her balance. She swings into Cooper, who catches her with a solid arm around the waist. Neither moves, not even once Martha regains her balance, and she's reminded of a time in seventh grade when Danny McCormick's knee found hers under the table and they sat frozen in that position for what seemed like a slow-motion hour, pretending that the contact was neither intentional or remarkable, though at the time an electric current ricocheted through Martha's body.

"Have you and Lucy ever discussed making Man Camp real?" Cooper asks, acting nonchalant about his arm. "I haven't stopped thinking about it since you mentioned it. It's brilliant. Hare-brained, to be sure, but full of possibilities."

Funny you should mention hair, Martha thinks, wanting to run her fingers through his mop. "I came up with the idea," she says in a low voice, immediately feeling silly for trying to take credit.

"That doesn't surprise me one bit," Cooper says, giving her a smile. "You know, Tuckington Farm has Man Camp written all over it."

"Seventy-ninth Street," Lucy calls out, spinning back around to catch her friends pressed together like statues, their faces close enough to kiss. "Almost there," she mumbles inaudibly.

Cooper lets his arm fall and Martha takes a baby step to one side.

"Would you believe this nut wants to make Man Camp real?" Martha says.

Lucy doesn't reply. That nut is my oldest friend, she thinks. He's *my* nut!

"I mean, he's serious, Luce," she continues. "He wants to create a real Man Camp at Tuckington Farm."

Give me a break, Lucy thinks.

"It's a great idea," Cooper says. "And I'm always in need of a few extra farmhands in the spring." He smiles at Martha. "My ulterior motive, of course, is to get you two down to the farm."

Lucy glares at his profile. *You're my backup plan! Why are you flirting with Martha?*

"Besides, can you imagine how much fun it would be to watch city boys become real men?" he asks.

"You might actually be onto something," Martha says, studying Cooper's calloused fingers wrapped around the pole in front of her. She wonders if the sense of accomplishment that vigorous outdoor work gives men might not be the relaxation equivalent of what spas do for women. Could it boost their confidence? Give them a jolt of endorphins? "Man Camp might be just what my FirstDate clients need. One date sure isn't cutting it. What do you think, Luce?"

"I don't know," Lucy answers, annoyed that she feels jealous.

"Well, I say the idea has great potential," Martha says. "Just think, if Man Camp works at the farm, we could franchise it."

"You might be right," Cooper says.

Lucy folds her arms across her chest.

Martha becomes giddy with the possibility. "Man Camps could sprout up all over the country," she says. "We could even have themes: Old Man Camp, Artsy Man Camp, Brainy Man Camp, Gay Man Camp . . ."

"Am I the only one who thinks this is a little on the man-bashing side?" Lucy asks. "To say nothing of an unlikely business venture."

"Might I remind you that I made a real go of FirstDate, an equally unlikely gambit?"

Cooper's eyes light up. "This could be a real moneymaker."

Lucy hadn't thought of Man Camp as an improved and expanded FirstDate, a way for men to do well with women. Then again, she'd never thought of making it real, period. The biologist in her knows that the promise of improving a male's chance at mating will always be desirable to him, though she's not ready to admit that Man Camp could work.

Cooper chuckles. "Come on, Luce. Think how easy it would be. All we need are some counselors and campers. We already have the perfect campsite."

"Tuckington Farm: home of the manly man!" Martha says, imitating what she imagines would be the voice-over for the Man Camp ad campaign.

Lucy isn't in the mood to be pitched.

"The three of us would make excellent counselors," Cooper says. "You two could teach lessons on chivalry and courtship, and I could show them how to plow fields and build fences, which would have the added bonus of helping me during my busiest season."

"What about the campers, Cooper?" Lucy asks in her dripping-with-patience voice, the one she usually reserves for freshmen with stupid questions.

"Look around you," Cooper says, his eyes landing on two young men who are seated nearby, chatting away, either oblivious or indifferent to the weary, pregnant woman clinging to the handrail above them. "Our campers are everywhere."

"Just because they're everywhere doesn't mean that Man Camp will be an easy sell," Lucy says. "Who in his right mind is going to sign up for it?"

"Well, obviously we wouldn't call it 'Man Camp' to their faces," Cooper says, sounding slightly exasperated. "But any guy who's willing to take dating classes isn't going to split hairs over this."

Point taken, Lucy thinks, but she's still not convinced.

Cooper's face grows boyish with enthusiasm. "Think, Lucy, you'd finally get to see Tuckington Farm and we'd be doing a good deed in the process. Those poor sorry sacks need our help."

Martha jumps in. "Why don't you bring Adam along? He stands to benefit as much as anyone else, plus it could be a vacation for you guys. Besides, it would be easy to convince him."

"Are you crazy?" Lucy says. But she hadn't considered that particular Man Camp benefit before. Presto, Adam might actually learn how to build a fire and chop wood. She pictures him in Levi's lifting big bales of hay off a truck, his smooth, brown arms corded with muscles.

"You could talk him into it," Cooper says. "Don't underrate your feminine wiles."

Lucy winces.

"All I mean is that you're incredibly persuasive," he explains. "If you told me to stand on the West Side Highway for an hour, I wouldn't even ask why."

Instead of being charmed, Lucy finds Cooper's speil disingenuous and irritating, and considers banishing him to the highway. "What you don't seem to get, Cooper, is that the men here aren't like you."

"Exactly why we need to send them to Man Camp!" He

smiles patiently. "There're two basic traits common to all men. One, we like to please women. Two, we like to please women. Admittedly, our reasons can be less than noble, but I guarantee you if you're clear with us, we'll always try to please you."

Lucy smiles back and sends a clear telepathic message: *You could please me by not falling in love with my best friend!* But part of her recognizes the truth in what Cooper's saying: she rarely lets Adam in on her needs because she's always so busy trying to figure out and accommodate his. If he's having a tough time with his dissertation (always), she takes care of the domestic chores. If he's struggling financially (often), she pays his half of the rent or picks up the tab for dinner. If he can't sleep (occasionally), she runs her fingers through his hair until his breathing grows deep.

They're almost at One Hundredth Street when Martha realizes they've missed their stop. "Whoops!" she says, grabbing Cooper's hand and pushing through the crowd. Lucy trails a few steps behind.

Once outside, the three of them get their bearings and reassemble themselves: button coats, wrap scarves, put on hats and gloves. They didn't overshoot the museum by much and it's a sunny day, windy but bearable, so they decide to walk.

Cooper offers each of them an arm. "Let's do this, you two," he says, squeezing their hands snugly between his arm and his body. "Seems to me, there's something in it for each of us." He looks at Lucy. "Adam becomes a fire-building, engine-repairing, fearless, swashbuckling outdoorsman." Then at Martha. "Man Camp is FirstDate on steroids and your clients get the intensive training they need, and you make buckets of money. And as for me, I get free labor for Tuckington Farm."

"Count me in," Martha says, tightening her grip on his bicep.

Lucy wants to object, not to Man Camp per se, but to how quickly everything's changing. Once an inside joke between best friends, Man Camp is fast becoming the vehicle by which Cooper and Martha are bonding without her. How soon before she becomes the third wheel? *Stop!* she tells herself, realizing she's on a downward spiral. *You have Adam. You don't need a backup. Why are you begrudging your two best friends a little fun?*

—

When they get to the museum, they stop alongside a row of vendors selling T-shirts, hats, and tiny replicas of Guggenheim paintings, one of which catches Lucy's eye: a vividly colored miniature of Picasso's "Woman with Yellow Hair." The woman in the painting has a rapturous expression on her face and her blonde, ponytailed head is cradled in her arms; she's asleep. "I need to go home and take a nap," Lucy says, unable to come up with a better excuse to leave them alone on Cooper's last day.

Her friends raise polite objections, but the decision is made. Cooper promises to call her as soon as his plane touches down in Virginia and Lucy gives him a long hug.

"No sad good-byes," he says, holding Lucy's shoulders in his hands. "And please consider Man Camp. If nothing else, it's an excuse to get together soon."

Lucy buries her hands deep in her pockets and watches Cooper and Martha disappear into the museum. Then she walks into Central Park, where the cold air is invigorating and her mind starts to clear. As she thinks about creating a real Man Camp, the idea starts to make more sense, especially the part about bringing Adam. She smiles at the thought of having all sorts of strange men together under one wide-open sky. What would a man like the tightly wound software tycoon possibly say to Martha's klutzy, young chef or to her neurotic brother?

And yet, the concept is pretty straightforward. Their goal will be to teach the campers how to be good men without having them feel as if they're being taught, make them capable without revealing the extent of their ineptitude, increase their masculinity without drawing attention to their lack of it.

The wind gusts and Lucy tucks her head down, watching long-dead leaves lift from the earth. Her feet sink slightly into the thawing ground, reminding her spring is on its way with the promise of renewal and hope. Soon, she thinks, addressing a stark elm tree, you'll have about three million leaves. She looks down at the ground. *And then inchworms will make their vertical migration.* Her pace quickens. *And then robins will appear, hopping along after the worms, and all the other birds will follow, and the frenetic mating rituals will begin.* Lucy closes her eyes and pictures the spectacular aerial courtships of ravens and eagles, the frenzied drumming of grouses' wings, the jolly, come-love-me songs of wrens, chickadees, and wood thrushes.

What might Adam do to woo her? Is Man Camp the place to find out?

COOPER BUYS TWO admission tickets, and he and Martha take the elevator to the top of the museum and wend their way down. Despite first meeting three years ago, they've never been alone before and getting a real conversation going without Lucy's presence is more difficult than either expects.

"You a baseball fan?" Cooper asks, reigning in a ridiculous grin.

"Is that the one with the hoops?" Martha jokes. She starts to tell him about her crazy cat and then stops, realizing that a man whose livelihood depends on the utility of domesticated animals might not think highly of such an ill-behaved pet.

"Cats love me," he says.

Not mine, she thinks.

Cooper tells her that dawn is his favorite time of day, and Martha recalls the handful of sunrises she's seen, always in a bleary-eyed state after a night on the town.

"I'm not much of a morning person, myself," Martha tells him, admitting that she's never changed the default setting on her alarm clock from noon. "Of course, usually I'm awake before that. Usually."

This is unfathomable to Cooper—a farmer's day is half over by noon—and he steers the conversation toward the safe topic of food. "Do you like to cook?" he asks. "I'm a sucker for all-American comfort foods: pancakes with maple syrup, mac and cheese, steak and potatoes."

Martha tries to conceal her horror. Alcohol notwithstanding, she hasn't knowingly touched a carbohydrate in months. Her refrigerator is packed with prepared foods: tiny six-packs of nonfat yogurts, hermetically sealed sprout salads, lean entrées ordered from nearby restaurants.

"What's your specialty?" he asks.

"The tuna and yellowtail sashimi combo at 212-GOJAPAN," Martha deadpans. "I give it my own flair by ordering extra ginger and wasabi."

During the course of their herky-jerky conversation, they wander down two full loops of the museum's spiral, passing an array of abstract paintings by Pollock, Kandinsky, and Rauschenberg, art that Martha doesn't particularly like. The museum is warm and she starts to feel queasy. Why aren't they goofing around at Wollman Rink or eating dim sum in Chinatown?

When they come upon a series of canvases painted solid white, she wants to joke: "I think someone hung those upside down," but instead says, "What do you think the artist is trying to convey?" Appalled to hear her mother's hostess-speak come out of her mouth, Martha wonders if she's sounding like a Stepford date, and smells anxiety rising from her sweater.

Her mother's voice reminds her not to slouch.

I'm fucked, Martha thinks and hears her mother *tsk-tsk*ing. She straightens up and looks around, certain she's headed toward a full-blown panic attack, and only dimly aware of the drone of Cooper's voice, dutifully answering her question—*blah, blah, minimalism, blah, derivative, blah, vitality.* She concentrates on her breathing.

"You okay?" Cooper asks. "Martha?"

Martha shakes her head. "Sorry, I'm a little spaced out."

"That's all right," he says. "What do you think of this one?"

Standing in front of an ugly painting with spatters of red over black and brown streaks, Martha tips her head to one side as if a compelling thought might slide out more easily that way. She stares hard at the painting. Her mother's voice advises her to tell Cooper she finds it interesting, but Martha reminds herself of the thousands of dollars she spent on therapy precisely to get away from her mother's brand of man-pleasing femininity. "The truth is I don't like abstract art. I know, I'm an actress, I live in New York, therefore I'm supposed to love all things cultural. What can I tell you? I like representational stuff: portraits, still lifes, that kind of thing." She looks at Cooper, hoping not to see disappointment looking back at her.

Cooper laughs his big, loud laugh, which sounds even louder in the library-quiet museum. "In that case, let's go to the permanent collection," he says, taking her hand and steering them toward the Thannhauser Room, full of Impressionist and Post-impressionist paintings. "One of the things I love about you, Martha, is how you always say exactly what's on your mind."

Martha might have told Cooper exactly what was on her mind had she not focused on his use of the word *love. One of the things he loves about me.* She wonders what the other things might be and looks down at her feet, studying the uneven white rings of salt on her boots, remnants of winter.

Her last boyfriend, Elliot, had been stingy with love, doling it out in microscopic portions and taking it back in a hundred small ways. He admitted to loving Martha only once in their two-year relationship and it felt like an admission, as if loving her was a character flaw he could fight by the sheer strength of his will. The boyfriend before Elliot had the opposite problem: he'd rendered the word meaningless through overuse, making his love of her indistinguishable from his love of, say, Milk Duds. He loved his favorite sneakers, *The Daily Show,* steak with grilled onions, dirt bike riding, Martha, and sisal rugs.

Slightly giddy at the day's developments, Martha tries to center herself by focusing on the painting in front of her, a Cézanne still life with pears so succulent and ripe that she feels a pang of hunger akin to lust and almost tastes the sweetness of the fruit on her tongue. All at once she understands what Hemingway meant about appreciating these pears more on an empty stomach.

FIRST THING MONDAY MORNING, Martha decides to practice her persuasive skills on her brother. She figures having one camper in the bag—even if it's only Jesse—will not only boost her confidence, but might help sway subsequent prospects.

"Jesse McKenna's office," a chirpy voice answers.

"Hi, Kathy," she says to his assistant. "It's Martha."

There is a click, a pause, some music, and then Jesse's voice.

"Isn't ten-thirty a little early for you, Martha?"

"Perhaps a tad," she says, propping herself up on some pillows. She takes a gulp of coffee. Up until that moment, she didn't know which tack to take, enticement or fear, but Jesse's remark has given her an idea. "I'm only up this early because I had a terrible nightmare about you," she says. "I'm calling to see if you're okay."

Jesse's voice softens. "I'm totally fine, really."

"It all seemed so real," Martha says, becoming Meryl Streep in *Silkwood* as she conjures up the nightmare. "Some sicko writer was sending anthrax to all the editors who'd turned down his manuscript, and you were next on his list. The only way to save you was to get you out of the city, but I couldn't reach you."

Jesse happens to be in the process of assessing manuscripts, something he does every day by skimming the query letter and reading the first five pages or so, before deciding its fate, as well as the fate of its author. A potentially *unstable* author. Jesse clears his throat.

You're going to hell, Martha thinks, wondering if her brother's buying it. "I know it was just a dream, Jesse, but the problem with living in New York City is that anything can happen." That should get his attention, she thinks, pulling the blankets up to her chin. "I'm sure glad to be headed out of town."

"Where're you off to?" Jesse asks nervously.

Got him! thinks Martha. "To a beautiful dairy farm in rural West Virginia," she says. "Remember Lucy's friend Cooper? I'm going down to his dairy farm to check out country living for a week and I'm taking some of my FirstDate clients along as a continuing-education program of sorts."

"Really? When are you leaving?"

"Whenever I can get things lined up with the guys, but probably not before the first or second week of May." She pauses for a moment to bait her trap. "I have an idea: Why don't you come, too? You could use a vacation."

LUCY IS CATCHING UP with Eva when Martha pushes through La Luna's red doors, cell phone attached to her ear. "Coffee tomorrow would be great," she says into the receiver, mouthing, *Kurt Becker,* to Lucy. "Okay. Three P.M. Café Blasé." She snaps the phone shut. "Another one-month follow-up scheduled. I'm all over Man Camp!" she announces, kissing Lucy on the cheek and immediately wiping off the lipstick mark. "I've called about a dozen FirstDate clients and already have one confirmed yes, three maybes, and lots of coffees scheduled."

"No no's?" Lucy asks, surprised.

"Oh, I've had no's," Martha says, "plenty of no's. My beer-spilling chef is studying for his pastry finals in May. My Zen vegetarian can't stomach animal husbandry. My wall climber is back with his girlfriend." She sits on the stool next to Lucy and waves hello to Eva, who is busy with another customer. "What can I say? Getting someone to give up a week of hard-earned vacation isn't easy, but we'll get there. How about you? Have you talked to Adam yet?"

Lucy shakes her head. She hasn't even broached the topic with him. "I've never lied to Adam before," she says solemnly.

"Oh, please!" Martha unbuttons her jacket. "There's a world of difference between a lie of omission and one of deception."

"You think?"

"Sure. If I didn't believe that, how could I sleep after concocting an anthrax nightmare to scare Jesse into coming?"

"So Jesse is our one-and-only yes?"

Martha nods.

"I missed you guys last week," Eva says, pouring Martha a Chardonnay. "How was your date with Fred?"

It takes Martha a moment to place the name. "Oh, Fred. He was nice."

Eva lifts one of her delicate eyebrows. "What didn't you like about him?"

"I guess maybe we didn't really click is all."

"Well, *you* might not have clicked," Eva tells her, leaning over the bar. "But I hung out with Fred after pottery class and let me tell you, he clicked. He *really* clicked."

How's that possible? Martha wonders, suddenly filled with dread. Could there be karmic implications for her not clicking with Fred? Might it mean that her click with Cooper was one-way, too?

Lucy sees Martha's panic. "Don't worry. Cooper likes you. Believe me, I could tell. He's a flirt, of course, and so polite you'd never know if he didn't like someone, but he lit up around you in a way I've never seen before."

Do I have a thought bubble over my head? Martha wonders.

"Want to let me in on what's going on?" Eva asks.

"Martha's got a crush on my oldest friend."

Eva says a singsongy, "Uh-oh."

"No uh-oh's. I'm happy about it. I think maybe there's always been a little spark there," Lucy says, but Eva's pursed lips let Lucy know she's not buying it, and Lucy changes the subject. "Our other big news is that we've decided to hold a real Man Camp on Cooper's farm."

"That's it," Eva says, slapping her rag down on the counter. "If you two ever skip another Monday, you're cut off." She walks to the other end of the bar.

"Are you worried about how to approach Adam about Man Camp?" Martha asks.

"Right now, I'm more worried that I'm going to kill him if he doesn't finish his dissertation. His writer's block is completely consuming him. He has no time for fun, no time for me, and especially no time to help out around the apartment."

"Well, he *is* a guy, after all."

"Why does that make it okay?"

"It doesn't, it's just a fact."

"When Adam moved in, he billed himself as a liberal, equality-minded boyfriend, willing to share all domestic responsibilities. That's what I signed on for."

"Darling, when in the history of men and women have you ever heard of a truly equitable distribution of domestic duties?" Martha asks.

Lucy shrugs.

Martha touches her friend's wrist. "We all think it's going to be different for us, but men just aren't hardwired the way we are."

Lucy can't wait until Cooper gets a cold and needs to be taken care of like a child, then maybe Martha won't be so calm in the face of male helplessness. "Has it ever struck you as odd that women are never the ones with spare time to watch football or play in some lame band? Every woman I know is like a lioness. When she's not taking care of cubs, she's out stalking and hunting gazelles for some loudmouth lion who sits on his haunches and roars for dinner."

"Luce, you have to pick your battles," Martha says. "Masculinity or domesticity? I suggest you stay focused on masculinity because the chances are slim that Adam will ever do his share of household chores. But, if you send him to Man Camp, he at least might learn to kill things for you."

Lucy laughs. "And you don't think it's wrong to not let him know the truth?"

"Of course it's wrong, it's just not wrong-wrong. We Catholics are good at gradations of sins and this would hardly count as a freckle on the back of a venial sin," Martha says, swirling the wine in her glass. Then she says, "Are you sure you don't mind that I like Cooper?"

"I'm getting used to the idea," Lucy says. "What happened after I left you two at the museum?"

"Cooper didn't tell you?"

"Of course he did. I just want to hear your version."

It's all the encouragement Martha needs. Her eyes light up as she thinks about their afternoon at the Guggenheim. "We mooned around each other like love-struck teenagers all day, but would you believe he never even suggested going back to my place?"

Of course he didn't, Lucy thinks. Cooper would want Martha to see Tuckington Farm first. "You've found your weaverbird in that man."

I've found my weaverbird, Martha thinks and pictures Cooper standing in front of Tuckington Farm with all its barns and silos and cows and pastures in the background, waving to her from inside the fence, beckoning her toward him.

LUCY SPENDS MOST OF the night skimming along the surface of sleep, alighting on the isthmus between consciousness and unconsciousness. She has a strange dream about the midair mating ritual of the honeybee, who mutilates himself by breaking off his genitalia inside the queen bee, leaving behind a chastity belt of sorts. Despite the soothing sounds of Adam's soft snores, she can't find the path back to sleep. Agitated, her brain flits from problem to problem, real and imaginary: she solves a dilemma in her research paper, argues with her mother, worries about a dinner party, plans a lecture, and rationalizes why it's okay not to tell Adam he's being drafted to go to Man Camp.

Finally, finally, finally, morning comes.

It's almost noon by the time Lucy gets off the train at 116th Street and walks purposefully toward the biology building. Somewhere in the midst of last night's nonsleep, she concluded that it was okay to let Adam believe he'd be more counselor than camper at Tuckington Farm. Martha was right, it didn't amount to a serious breach of trust. Besides, Lucy plans to make sure that Adam has the vacation of a lifetime: romantic walks, horseback rides, lovemaking under the stars.

Lucy navigates the maze of space that makes up the biology department: ten floors of offices, labs, and libraries; corridors humming with activity; machines that shake, shift, and spin in order to separate, grow, and divide their contents. She passes a special freezer tank, home to hundreds of tissue samples and millions of cells, and makes a quick stop at the cold room to deposit a brown lunch bag full of Adam's favorite delicacies beside some incubating proteins.

Lucy's Pavlovian plan is to follow every mention of Tuckington Farm with a treat: dairy cows, a slice of apple with Brie; silos, some champagne; tractors, a heartfelt kiss; and so on. She hopes that Cooper's assertion about men wanting to please women is right, and that Adam will want to please her *without* a lot of questions. The office picnic, conceived of before dawn, is designed to facilitate this instinct in her boyfriend.

Decorated in institutional furnishings, Lucy's office is drab and depressing save for the old slate blackboard behind her desk. On it is a large graph Adam drew in blue chalk two years ago on the day he first told Lucy that he loved her. His graph illustrated how their love would grow over time: a solid, straight line traveling upward in perpetuity. Lucy chalked her own love theory on top of his in red: a soaring peak followed by a long, slow descent.

"I'll prove you wrong," Adam said, and at the time, she almost believed he would.

Back then, Lucy found Adam's forgetfulness and social awkwardness charming, proof of his brilliance. Now, she just wishes he'd keep a to-do list and pay more attention. She wants him to start behaving like the male of any nonhuman species—proud like a peacock, powerful like a bull, possessive like a blue milkweed beetle—and prove to her he's the best man for the job of her mate.

Lucy puts some daisies in a mug, lays a blanket out on the floor, and tries to will herself into a romantic mood. But the image of Adam the night before, reading an economics book in striped boxer shorts and droopy black socks, his stomach relaxing out over his waistband, is stuck in her mind. Why is this what I'm settling for? she wonders. Why not for the poet who wrote movingly of his love for me, or the millionaire who wanted to pamper me, or any number of balding men who were willing to work harder because they had to?

A knock pulls her out of her thoughts and Adam's face peeks around the door. She's struck by how handsome she finds him; each time it surprises her anew.

He looks pleased at the sight before him: Lucy stretched out on the sofa in a soft, gray sweater with a curious smile on her face. But he instantly becomes nervous, as if calculating whether or not he's forgotten an important date. "What's the occasion?"

"No occasion," she says, getting up to kiss him. As their lips touch, she runs her fingers up the back of his neck into his hairline, activating goose bumps. "It just occurred to me that we haven't had an office picnic in forever," she says, pressing her body against his, hoping to remind him of their last office picnic, months ago now, when they ended up making achingly quiet love on the floor, oblivious to the activity just on the other side of her door: scientists hunching over microscopes, cells growing under the sterile hoods of incubators, petri dishes rocking back and forth on swaying apparatuses.

Lucy excuses herself to retrieve their picnic from the cold room and when she returns, brown bag in hand, she can tell that her embrace has had its intended memory jolt. She hands him a bottle of champagne to open, sits on the blanket, places a slab of Brie on a hunk of bread, and feeds it to him. She runs her fingers through his hair and watches Adam's eyes close in pleasure.

"Honey," she says softly, tracing a line of kisses along his jaw. "I'd like us to go to Tuckington Farm next month for a vacation." She puts a Dixie cup of champagne to his lips.

"Sure, baby," he says, blissed out, waiting for the next morsel of food or kiss.

Sure, baby? Lucy thinks. That's all there is to it? She feels a bit like Dorothy from *The Wizard of Oz* upon learning she's had the power to get back to Kansas all along. Why has she spent all these years trying to give men what they want and accept them as they are? Apparently, everyone else knows it doesn't work like that. It's about negotiating and bargaining and sex; even Cooper said as much.

"Great," she says, stroking his shoulders. "We're going to have a fantastic time."

"Mm," Adam agrees, still in his love daze.

"Cooper says we'll be in time for calving," she tells him. "And Martha's going to bring some of her FirstDate guys along for a little postgrad work."

Adam's eyes pop open at the mention of FirstDate. "Ugh.

It's so pathetic that men would sign up for that," he says.

Lucy stands up quickly, hitting her funny bone against the corner of the table. "It's not pathetic," she says, rubbing her elbow. "They just need a little help. No shame in that, right?" She walks over to the blackboard. "You still think your graph is right and mine is wrong?"

"The truth probably lies somewhere in between," Adam says. "Our love is probably more like the stock market. We have ups and downs, rallies and adjustments, but overall, there's a strong upward trend."

Lucy smiles and hopes he is right.

CHAPTER 8

"On the one hand, we'll never experience childbirth. On the other hand, we can open all our own jars."

Bruce Willis

COOPER IS WAITING for the campers and counselors just outside baggage claim at the Roanoke Regional Airport, where he greets them warmly: kisses for Lucy and Martha, handshakes for recruits Simon Hodges, Kurt Becker, Walter Sherman, and Bryce Carroll, and insider handshakes for Jesse and Adam, whose special status he acknowledges with a knowing look. Wearing old blue jeans, a flannel shirt, and a well-worn leather jacket, Cooper tosses the men's bags onto the flatbed of his truck, hurrying them along so they'll have daylight for the drive. The Manasseh Valley, home to Tuckington Farm, is due west beyond the walls of the Blue Ridge and Allegheny mountains.

The truck, an enormous Dodge pickup with an extended quad cab, two sets of doors, and double wheels in the rear, couldn't be less inviting. It's dented and covered in mud, with grimy windows and two bench seats that look as if they might comfortably seat six. There are nine in their group.

Ready to step up as the alpha male, Kurt says, "There isn't room for all of us in there," and announces that he's going to rent a car.

"No need to do that," Cooper tells him, flinging the last of the bags on board. "The girls will be riding with my mother. She's just running a little late on her errands, but she'll be here soon."

Cooper hustles Lucy and Martha toward the designated meeting spot just inside the terminal, guiding them with a hand on each of their elbows. When Lucy glances back and sees Adam looking bewildered by her hasty departure, she tries to slow down, upset that she hasn't had the chance to explain what's going on to him, but Cooper keeps them marching forward at a steady clip. Martha also looks over her shoulder to check on her brother. He's fine, leaning against the truck, uncharacteristically oblivious to its dirt, a result of the antianxiety medication that enabled him to get on the plane in the first place.

It was Cooper's idea to separate the men and the women early on, an idea that Lucy hadn't been too happy about, but one he convinced her would be psychologically advantageous. "We won't be able to bond if I can't get them outside of their comfort zone and in touch with their survival instincts," he told her over the phone. "It's just how it works with men."

But now that they're back inside the terminal and Adam's out of sight, Lucy gets anxious. "Isn't Adam going to get suspicious about why he's riding with the campers and not with us?"

"I'll be with him, Lucy. I'll make sure he thinks he's a counselor, don't worry," Cooper says, still holding her elbow. "Now, if you really want to help him, you have to stop being so protective."

Annoyed, Lucy wriggles out of his grasp and wanders back toward the doors to watch the men through the glass. Cooper takes advantage of the moment to talk to Martha. "I don't think I've ever been gladder to be me than I am at this moment," he says, smiling at her.

Staring through the sliding glass doors, Lucy wonders if Adam is upset with her. He appears to be doing okay, though, chatting with Walter, the obnoxious camper who distinguished himself by hitting on the flight attendant. She feels like a mother spying on her child at the playground, but when she catches Walter maneuvering Adam into the truck first so he can save a window seat for himself, the blood rises to her cheeks. Adam gets carsick easily, after all. And what if the first lesson he learns at Man Camp is how to be a womanizer?

"He'll be fine, Luce," Cooper says gently, talking to her in the reassuring tones of an older brother. "No more security blankets, remember? Adam is in Man Camp now." He smiles. "I'll see you ladies at the farm."

Lucy and Martha watch as Cooper and the men prepare to leave. It's obvious even from this distance that they are nervous, trying to impress one another and establish some pecking order. Kurt is having an animated conversation on his cell phone, no doubt barking orders to some underling back in New York on how to handle whatever strategic strikes and insurgencies occur in his absence. Bryce is busy rearranging his Louis Vuitton leather suitcase, wedging it between two other bags so that no part of it is in contact with Cooper's filthy truck. Simon has a map of the region spread open on the hood of the vehicle and is dragging his finger along the route they'll be taking over the Alleghenies, listing historically significant sites to an inattentive audience. And it looks like Walter is tapping out messages on his Blackberry, though he could be playing with his GameBoy or downloading porn, all the while reserving his seat by sitting half in and half out of the truck.

"Ready, fellas?" Cooper shouts over the noisy rattling of the Dodge's diesel engine. Beside him in the front are Jesse and Kurt, with Bryce, Simon, Adam, and Walter packed tightly in the back. "If it's okay with y'all, I'm going to do my best to avoid the city."

"What city?" Bryce whispers to Simon. "There are only four real cities in the world: New York, Paris, Rome, and London. Roanoke is barely a village." He kicks a greasy tool that has slid out from under the front seat and looks at his shoe to see if he dirtied the toe. "Any chance we pass a Starbucks en route?"

Ignoring the question, Cooper rolls down his window and watches with some amusement in the rearview mirror as Bryce's hands fly up to protect his hair from the wind. He must be the metrosexual, Cooper thinks.

Walter brags to the campers about a segment he produced for NBC on Amish farmers. "Once you've spent two weeks in rural Pennsylvania using a walking plow pulled by a team of horses, pretty much all other farm life seems cushy."

"I hope that'll be the case for you," Cooper says, smiling. He drives with one hand on the wheel and the other hanging out of the truck, hammering a ditty on the door that he'd like to play on his guitar for Martha: *Lavender blue, dilly dilly, lavender green/ If I were king, dilly dilly, I'd need a queen.* In no time, he has them on State Route 311, a two-lane road edged by forests of oak, maple, and walnut trees, which starts flat but soon undulates in the hilly countryside. "Hang on," he tells them, stepping on the gas and passing traffic with little concern for oncoming vehicles, inadvertently whacking Jesse in the knee with the gear stick each time he shifts into second or fourth.

Simon, silent up until now, clears his throat and leans forward from the backseat to announce that he's spent the last few weeks reading up on the Manasseh Valley region and its history. "I tell you this merely to inform you that I've become something of an expert on all things Appa-LAY-chian, should any of you have any questions."

Cooper winces at Simon's Yankee pronunciation and corrects him gently: "We say Appa-LAH-chian around here." His voice is kind and patient.

"Oh, yes. Right. Of course," Simon says, clearing his throat again, a nervous tick. "I just love local dialects. Are you aware that the language here has its roots in Elizabethan English?" With another few coughs, Simon is off and running, talking a steady stream about the virtues of Southern phraseology. "One of my absolute favorite things is the charming use of double negatives for emphasis. It's so classical Greek."

The group exchange glances charged with the solidarity that comes with finding a common enemy.

Feeling queasy from the hills and turns, and bored by Simon's pontificating, Adam shuts his eyes and drifts off to the comforting land of equations, where he considers the variables necessary to do a cost-benefit analysis of Martha's new business venture. He has little information to go on other than the knowledge that the participants in the trial run are paying approximately five hundred dollars each (for airfare and food), and that the goal of the program is to make the men more successful with women. Assuming it works, the most important number Adam needs to determine is the money saved by *having* a girlfriend versus *trying to secure one.* To do that, he calculates the cost of "early" dating (arguably the most expensive time in any relationship, with its requisite fancy dinners, cabs, flowers, and gifts) and compares it with the costs of being in a relationship (when it becomes acceptable to do things on the cheap like rent a video and order in Chinese food). He makes an educated guess at the overall reduction in the number of dates that a "graduate" of the program will have to go on before securing a mate—three—and he plugs that into his calculations. As much as he hates to admit it, if Martha can shave just three or more women off a man's dating portfolio before meeting Ms. Right, the potential to optimize the return on his investment will more than justify the hefty tuition she hopes someday to charge.

MARTHA GUESSED WRONG when she imagined that Cooper's mother would have apple-round cheeks, hair tied back in a loose bun, and smell vaguely of cinnamon and brown sugar. Beatrice, who pulls up in a silver Saab convertible, is whippet thin, dressed in snug jeans and a plunging sweater.

"Lucy Stone!" Beatrice calls as she gets out of her car. "Is it possible that you've grown more beautiful since I saw you last?" She kisses the air next to Lucy's cheeks. "I don't know how I can ever forgive Cooper for letting you get away!"

Get away? Martha thinks.

Lucy blushes, unsure of how to respond. She's only met Beatrice on one other occasion, the night of Cooper's graduation, and, if she recalls correctly, Beatrice was anything but subtle in expressing her displeasure over Lucy's presence at their family gathering. "It's good to see you again, Beatrice," Lucy says. "I'd like you to meet my best friend, Martha McKenna."

"So, you're Martha," Beatrice says, stepping back to give her an appraising look, which reveals that Martha is *not* what she was expecting. "But I was sure Cooper said that you were an actress."

"I am," Martha says, desperate to come up with an interpretation for the comment other than that Beatrice doesn't think she's pretty enough to be an actress. "It's nice to finally meet you." Martha takes Beatrice's right hand in both of hers, a gesture that is meant to be warm, but comes across as supplicating.

Of course it is, Beatrice smiles back. Then she turns back to Lucy. "Cooper has kept me updated on your every move over the years and I can't wait to hear all about your fascinating career. It must be so fulfilling to do important work." She glances at Martha, who nods agreeably.

Beatrice opens the trunk of the convertible, which is jampacked with groceries, and places Lucy's computer bag inside. "I'm afraid the rest will have to go in the back with you," she says to Martha.

WHEN ADAM OPENS HIS EYES, they have left the Catawba Valley, passed into the Thomas Jefferson National Forest, and are starting to cross the three huge ridges that separate Virginia from West Virginia, climbing and descending on roads that are a jumble of switchbacks and S-curves. He looks at the compass that's fixed to the dashboard. The pointer keeps changing directions, often indicating that they're heading due east, back the way they came. Every few miles they get stuck behind a huge lumber truck, piled high with chained-down logs, four feet wide at their trunks.

"I don't even want to know what would happen if one of those logs came unchained," Jesse says, slurring slightly from his antianxiety medication. Without a seat belt for the middle passenger, Jesse lists back and forth, unable to steady himself, even with both hands on the dashboard.

"We'd be sorrier than a cow on its way to McDonald's," Cooper says, stepping on the accelerator, trying to get around one of the hulking trucks. The Dodge's diesel engine cranks up slowly and the men hold their breath, praying no cars are coming in the other direction. Occasionally, the truck drivers politely pull over onto the shoulder to allow traffic to pass, but often there isn't a shoulder and more often the drivers aren't polite.

Kurt and Walter, who occupy the two passenger-side window seats, find themselves looking down steep escarpments onto the roofs of houses hundreds of feet below, drops that start just a few yards from the wheels of the truck. Every so often, there's a patch of aluminum guard railing that's either dented or completely torn through, but most of the time there's nothing between the truck and the precipitous drop. Walter put his GameBoy down miles ago, and clutches the armrest as he counts the markers, crosses and flowered wreaths in varying states of decay, memorializing where people have gone off the road and, presumably, to the hereafter.

On the other side of the road, the land rises straight up in great sheets of shiny rock. There's roadkill everywhere, more than any of them has ever seen on all their trips to the Hamptons combined: deer, groundhogs, skunks, possums, and other unrecognizable carcasses. Warning signs dot the road: WATCH OUT FOR FALLING ROCKS, BLIND CURVE, DEER CROSSING, NO PASSING. But Cooper ignores all of them as he speeds over the mountains, straightening out curves by crossing the double yellow lines.

On clear days, he tells them, there are vistas of astonishing beauty at the tops of each ridge, overlooking valleys with creeks running along the bottoms outlined in fingers of silver mist. But today it's overcast and low ceilings of clouds hover at the ridges, enveloping the truck in thick fog. When they're at the top of the third and final ridge, at an elevation of over three thousand feet, Cooper tells them they are crossing the spot where the water stops flowing east toward the Atlantic and begins flowing west toward the Ohio and Mississippi rivers, and ultimately into the Gulf of Mexico. Suddenly, the road falls out from underneath the campers and they plunge out of the clouds and into the valley, ears popping as they lose a thousand feet of elevation in minutes.

FOLDED INTO THE BACKSEAT of the Saab and squashed alongside their suitcases, Martha wishes she could peg what she finds unnerving about the diminutive woman who's driving the car. Instead, she and Lucy fill Beatrice in on everything about Man Camp, from the genesis of the idea at La Luna to what they hope to accomplish at Tuckington Farm.

"Our main goal is to masculinize pampered city boys," Martha explains.

"To help them find their inner man," Lucy adds.

"I have to admit, when Cooper first told me about this, I assumed he'd gotten it wrong," Beatrice says, laughing. "In my day, it was the women's job to take some of the manliness *out* of the men, not try to put any back *in.* I figured that the only reason you'd bring men down here was for refinement, to teach them something about how to become Southern gentlemen."

Lucy can only imagine how crazy it must sound to a woman like Beatrice, who has spent her life around capable men, men who hunt and farm and work with their hands. "You'll see what we're up against soon enough," she promises. "It's not that they're not great men; they really are. It's just that you wouldn't want to count on any of them in a crisis."

"Yep," Martha chimes in from the back, "there's nary a dragon slayer among them."

"What?" Beatrice says.

Martha repeats the joke and Beatrice says, "That's what I thought you said."

To change the subject, Lucy launches into the Man Camp training calendar for the week. "If Cooper's on schedule," she says, looking at her watch, "Man Camp training is officially about to begin."

"Automotive 101," Martha says. "Fixing a flat tire."

Lucy smiles at the prospect of Adam having grease on his hands. "Per our plan, Cooper is going to handle all the rudimentary macho stuff like carpentry, engine repair, farming, hunting, and so on. Our job will be to teach them the subtler art of masculinity: how to behave around women."

"And these men actually *know* why you've brought them here?" Beatrice asks.

"Every one of them signed up willingly!" Martha says.

Lucy looks back at Martha. "Well, not exactly *everyone,*" she says haltingly. "My boyfriend and Martha's brother are under the impression that they're here to support us."

"Nothing wrong with that," Beatrice assures her. "My philosophy has always been to give men information on a need-to-know basis."

Instead of feeling relieved, Lucy feels more anxious.

"We were thinking it might be fun to throw a party at the end of the week to celebrate their accomplishments," Martha says.

"And maybe invite lots of Southern belles so the campers

could practice their courtship skills," Lucy adds.

"That's a terrific idea. How about making it a dance?" Beatrice suggests.

"Even better," Martha says.

"The old barn is the perfect spot and Jolene can help organize."

"Jolene?" Martha asks.

"Yes, Jolene. She's such a dear and so talented!" Beatrice says. "She's a close friend of Cooper's from church."

Martha swallows hard.

IN A TOWN CALLED New Penial, Cooper announces that he needs to take a leak, and pulls the truck off the road beside a colonial ruin from the time of Thomas Jefferson. He leaps out of the car and, before the men even have a chance to open their doors, surreptitiously drops a couple of jack rocks in front of the rear wheel on the driver's side. Then he relieves himself in a ditch. "Just a short ways up the road, there's a big-ass statue commemorating the Confederate dead. The town fathers erected it one hundred years ago, assuming the settlement would expand north, only it never did and the poor thing stands out there, all by its lonesome, with nothing but horses grazing around it."

The men smile; it's hard not to like an affable guy like Cooper even though they were prepared not to. They already feel more at ease about their trip.

Simon gives his warning cough and starts an impromptu lecture on the Civil War. "Perhaps not everyone here knows that in 1862, Lincoln signed a bill creating the state of West Virginia to enlist its citizens to help the Union side."

Cooper starts the engine and carefully drives over the newly planted jack rocks. Within a few miles, the campers hear the unfamiliar *thunk-thunk* sound of deflated rubber.

"Looks like we got us a flat, boys," Cooper says, pulling over onto the shoulder and waiting for all the men to pile out.

Kurt points to the mass of nails sticking out from the tire. "What the hell is that?"

"That, my friend, is called a jack rock," Cooper tells him. "It's made of bent nails welded together, so that however it lands, one of the nails is always pointing upward. Pretty insidious, huh? Miners used to use them in union disputes to wreck the tires of the scab workers' vehicles and the coal trucks, but this one was probably some kid's idea of a prank."

"Speaking of union disputes, it would be great to talk to some of the locals about the labor struggles of the twenties and thirties," Simon says. "Perhaps there are some establishments where I could—"

"First things first," Cooper interrupts. "We've got a tire to fix."

"I got us covered here, gentlemen," Walter announces, whipping out his cell phone and Palm Pilot. "AAA guarantees service in less than half an hour for its premier members." He assumes his best premier-member stance, legs shoulder-width apart, and taps the tiny buttons on his various gadgets.

There's a palpable sense of relief among the men.

A moment passes and Walter gives his phone a look of consternation. He *shh*es Cooper, who's trying to get his attention, and punches more buttons.

"Sorry, friend," Cooper says, pointing to the wall of mountains. "You're not going to get a signal anywhere near here."

Walter shuts the phone.

"Don't feel bad," Cooper says. "Even if there was a signal, there isn't a service station for miles. The good news is you'll get cell coverage on the farm."

A pall is cast upon the group.

Kurt says, "What the hell are we going to do now?" The vein in his forehead pulses with rage.

"It's a flat, for God's sake," Cooper says, genuinely surprised at their helplessness. He'd been thirteen the first time he'd fixed a flat alone and even then it came as naturally as milking cows; he knew what to do from years of observing his father. Didn't these city guys have dads? Or was there just never anything to fix in the city? "We get flats all the time in this terrain," Cooper says, snapping back to the business at hand. "It's no big deal. Hell, even if we didn't have everything we needed to fix it, there're *seven* of us! We could carry the truck if we had to." Cooper kneels down in the mud, looks under the vehicle, and assesses the damage.

Aghast, Bryce watches as stains spread across the knees of Cooper's jeans, the exact-vintage classic Levi's he's been in search of for over a year. "Where'd you get your jeans?" he asks, admiring the stitching. "I've looked for that pair in every vintage store in Manhattan!"

"They were my dad's, Bryce," Cooper says evenly. "Now, let's focus on learning a thing or two about how to change a tire. Adam, will you grab me the gauge from the glove box?"

When Adam opens the box, the first thing he comes upon is a shiny pistol. "Holy shit," he says, picking up the gun. "What's this doing here? Is it loaded?"

"Of course it's loaded," Cooper says. "You don't carry a gun because it's pretty. Now, put it down and grab the tire gauge, would you?"

Adam does as he's told. "Why do you have it?"

"No particular reason," Cooper answers. "Most people carry in these parts. It tends to keep trouble at bay. Maybe we'll do some shooting at the farm later in the week. Or better yet, I'll take y'all to the range."

As shocked as they were by the gun, Cooper can tell the idea of shooting somehow intrigues the campers. Clearly, he's tapped into the universal male desire to blow things up. "So when's the last time any of you changed a tire?" he asks.

Silence.

Cooper can't believe it—he owes Martha ten bucks! He didn't think it was possible that six grown men had never changed a tire. "You mean to tell me none of you has *ever* done this?" He looks at Adam and Bryce, who happen to be standing closest. "What do you do when your girlfriend calls with a flat?"

"Tell her to hail another cab?" Bryce says.

Not amused, Cooper says, "We take caring for our women seriously in these parts."

"It was just a joke," Bryce says. "The point is, no one drives in New York."

"And in our parts," Adam adds, "we'd be in more trouble for referring to them as 'our women.' "

Cooper likes that Adam has stood up to him, and imagines that he has a point to boot. Perhaps Cooper hasn't given him enough credit.

"Well, I don't think we'd want to hail anyone around here," Jesse adds, having noticed a certain *Deliverance*-like physiognomy in the truck drivers who've been passing them, with rifles stacked high on racks in their rear windows.

"You're right about that," Cooper says, thinking a little hillbilly fear might help motivate the men to learn. "Shall I show you how this goes?"

The campers give Cooper their full attention and make a tight semicircle around him.

"First thing you do is get your tire iron," he says, reaching under the driver's seat. "Which, incidentally, doubles as a weapon in a pinch." He slaps the tire iron against his hand to demonstrate its heft. "Then you loosen the lugs on the bum wheel. Now, a lot of guys will want to jack up the truck first, but you'll know better," Cooper says, lowering his voice. "You can't get traction if the wheel spins, so leave it on the ground and take advantage of leverage."

There are some *ahh*'s and *hmm*'s.

"Anyone want to take a shot at loosening the lugs?"

Kurt volunteers, though instead of following Cooper's suggestion to lean into it and use his body mass and legs for leverage, he puts his gym-toned biceps and shoulders to work, grunting from the strain.

"Good job," Cooper says, slapping Kurt on the back for praise. He can respect a man who finds his own way. He places the handful of lugs into Jesse's palm and tells him not to lose them.

One by one, Cooper gets each man involved and soon they are working as a team: Walter breaks out the jack; Bryce checks the pressure of the other tires; Adam goes under the truck to unchain the spare, which Cooper tells him is just past the rear differential. (He figures he'll know what a rear differential looks like once he's found the spare.)

Cooper shows them how to find the best spot on the frame for the jack, and using the lug wrench as a handle, Walter pumps the jack up and down until it lifts the truck, eventually bringing the tire off the ground. Of course, he can't resist the opportunity to exaggerate the thrusting motion, grunting away like a frat boy getting lucky. Cooper considers reprimanding him for his juvenile behavior, but decides against it. Lucy and Martha are in charge of manners, and he needs to stay focused on his own job: teaching the campers trademark acts of masculinity.

"Remember: the spare will have more volume than the flat," he tells them. "So make sure to lift the truck higher than you think you'll have to."

The men are getting into the lesson now, excited that Cooper is letting them in on tricks that would take years for them to figure out on their own.

Cooper pulls off the flat with a jerk and slides the spare expertly onto the hub. "You'll want to finger-tighten the lug nuts in a star pattern to hold the tire in place," he explains, "then you use the lug wrench to finish the job." Once the lugs are secure, he has Jesse reinsert the wrench into the jack and turn it a quarter turn. The cylinder lets off and the truck settles back to the ground.

"Cool," Jesse says.

"Now that it's back on the ground, you want to tighten them one last time," Cooper tells him.

At this very moment, Martha and Lucy and Beatrice drive by, slowing down to a stop about twenty feet in front of Cooper's truck when they see the men stranded. Martha sticks her head out the passenger-side window. "Everything okay?" she shouts.

Jesse's hand is still on the jack. "Everything's fine," he calls back, *No big deal* written all over his face. "Just changing a tire."

Cooper smiles and gives Martha a thumbs-up. "We'll be right behind you."

Adam waves to Lucy and calls out, "See you at the farm."

"Okey-dokey," Lucy says. "Dinner will be waiting."

As Beatrice accelerates, Lucy rolls up the window. She and Martha howl with laughter, thrilled that Man Camp is already working.

With the dirty work behind them, Bryce breaks out a handful of individually packaged sanitary wipes that he has stashed in his knapsack. " 'Be prepared' is my motto," he says, offering them to his new friends.

"One step forward, two steps back," mutters Cooper, wiping his own hands on the dirty rag he keeps under his seat.

The light is green when they finally drive into Neola, the county seat of Manasseh Valley, and Cooper slows down along the main drag, a narrow road framed by hundred-year-old trees. They pass the Neola County Courthouse, built in 1837, the old post office, and the barbershop where Cooper has gotten his hair cut his whole life. The sun has settled behind the hills and it's almost dark when they drive by the pond where Cooper skated as a child. Across from the pond is a Confederate cemetery and beyond that is Tuckington Drive, the long dirt road that leads to the eight-hundred-acre farm.

There's just enough light for the men to make out the edges of things: the main barn, which Cooper calls the Cow Palace, various sheds and shacks, a rickety fence outlining the perimeter, a silo, cows huddled together in clusters, bales of hay. But Cooper, who is as familiar with the farm as he is with his own body, sees something the men miss: a foreclosure notice freshly tacked to the fence that runs along the drive. Though the bank has sent many letters, he's sure he has at least another month or so before they take any action. Plenty of time, he thinks, to get things back on track. His heart races and he hopes his mother didn't notice the sign, which he'll remove after his guests are asleep.

When they arrive at the farmhouse, two golden retrievers run out to greet the truck. Cooper introduces them to the campers as Tor and Tap, explaining that there have always been two golden retrievers named Tor and Tap on the Tuckington property, a tradition Cooper's father and grandfather set into motion and one that Cooper has followed without questioning. "Not much as guard dogs," Cooper tells the men as they grab their bags, "but good company and loyal as bark is to trees."

Lucy and Martha and Beatrice pour out onto the porch looking like three haloed angels, backlit from the glow of lights in the kitchen. The delicious smells of roasted potatoes and chicken waft out behind them.

Beatrice steps forward and shakes hands with each of the campers as they file past her. "I'm awful glad to meet you," she says, exaggerating her Southern accent. When Cooper reaches her, she mock-scolds him for their benefit: "Cooper Tuckington, exactly what kind of a welcome is that for our guests?" She beams at him, patting his chest through the leather jacket. "Don't you think these handsome men have anything better to do with their time than help you change a tire?"

CHAPTER 9

"It's not the men in my life that counts—it's the life in my men."

Mae West

LITTLE COULD SEEM farther from the men's daily New York routine than life on Tuckington Farm. In the city, their lives take place roughly between 8 A.M. and midnight, and their schedules are all variations on a theme: they hit the snooze button a few times before waking to their favorite talk-radio program and enjoy morning rituals of showers, lattes, and newspapers; if they're motivated, they go to the gym; if not, they go directly to work, where they spend the next ten to twelve hours on e-mail and headsets; they pass most evenings in nice restaurants with friends, colleagues, or the occasional date, though sometimes they stay at home, order Chinese, and watch reality television.

Not so at Tuckington Farm. Here, with the help of a leghorn rooster named Pavarotti, Cooper wakes the men at 5 A.M., gives them a mug of Folgers, loads them onto the flatbed of one of his pickup trucks, and drives them to the milking parlor, a half mile from his house. There, disoriented and unshowered, the men stand on industrial rubber mats stretched along a sunken walkway between two raised platforms where, for the next ninety minutes, a steady stream of fourteen-hundred-pound cows are ushered through in batches of twenty-four, twelve per side.

The six campers, spaced evenly along the central corridor, are responsible for milking four cows at a time, two per side. Cooper makes a point of telling them how lucky they are to be in a state-of-the-art facility where the cow udders are at waist level and minimal stooping is required. They look at him bleary-eyed and annoyed, no doubt wondering how they got talked into coming to Tuckington Farm in the first place. "The job is usually handled by two farmhands," he tells them. "So it should be a piece of cake for you guys."

In a show of solidarity with the men, Lucy and Martha wake up at the same ungodly hour to observe the dairy operation from the front section of the building, where Cooper has set out two ancient milking stools. From this vantage point, they watch the cows march in wild-eyed, their bags so unnervingly full of milk that the large varicose veins running along the sides look as if they might pop off or explode.

The cows, already agitated by their physical state, are especially skittish in the presence of the unfamiliar men, and Cooper does his best to calm them. In a low, soft voice, he lectures the campers on how to handle livestock and equipment, occasionally interrupting himself to cluck encouragement to a startled cow and get her moving into her station.

"It's very important that we don't dip below our production goal of seventy-five hundred pounds of milk per day," he tells the campers. "That means hooking up the equipment properly and keeping everything as serene as possible in here. And remember, the cardinal rule in the dairy parlor is no hand-to-cow contact."

"Why's that?" Adam asks.

"Because it's unsanitary and the Department of Agriculture is particular about contaminants in the milk supply," Cooper replies sternly. Then he sees Lucy and Martha out of the corner of his eye and forces a smile. "They send inspectors—greasy little men with thick glasses and no chins, who we regularly kill and eat."

The men laugh at Cooper's joke and then watch him demonstrate how to milk a cow. He submerges each teat in a bottle of cleanser, wipes off the excess with a special cloth, and connects the teat to a device called "the claw" (the bovine equivalent of a breast pump), which has four suction attachments that pump the milk into individual six-gallon recording jars with red marks on the sides like those on measuring cups.

"How I wish I hadn't just seen him do that," Martha whispers to Lucy, crossing her arms over her breasts.

Not surprisingly, Kurt hooks his cows up the fastest and then makes the rounds, drill-sergeant-style, to rally the troops. He stops beside Bryce, who handles the claw with as little physical contact as possible. "It's not a bomb," Kurt tells him. "You're slowing us up here, buddy. Remember, there's no *I* in *team*!"

"There's a *Me*," counters Bryce, who seems content just to be the best-dressed dairy farmer of the bunch, wearing brand-new Carhartt overalls and L.L. Bean boots.

Nervous at being watched, Jesse gets his index finger stuck in one of the suction tubes of the claw, which provokes all sorts of snickers from Walter until Cooper turns off the machine to extricate Jesse's digit.

Simon is unusually quiet, which makes Martha wonder if

he's picked up on his unpopularity or if he (like her) just isn't a morning person. And Adam works at a steady clip, deftly hooking up his cows, whistling softly to keep them calm and happy.

Lucy, meanwhile, marvels at the contrast between the earthiness of the cows with their four gurgling stomachs, and the dairy's high-tech systems designed to measure, transport, and cool. Then she thinks of the lovely end result of all this activity: milk, white, pasteurized, and government approved for mass consumption by children.

Martha wonders aloud if the herd wouldn't be more at home listening to country music rather than the classical stuff that is being piped in from Cooper's office.

"It's all about relaxation," Cooper tells her, pulling up a third stool. "The more soothing the sounds are, the better the milk flows. Believe it or not, a dairy farm is a pretty cushy life for a cow."

Martha gives him a skeptical look. *Forced reproduction and breast pumping. Cushy?* She doesn't buy it. She knows from the back of the GOJAPAN takeout menu that Kobe cattle are given beer with their meals and massaged daily, which sounds more like the level of pampering she'd opt for if she were a cow.

When the last claw releases its grip on the last cow, the deflated four-legged ladies are led out of the far end of the parlor looking much more comfortable than when they arrived. Almost immediately a new bunch files in, brown eyes rolling wildly, bags about to burst.

Lucy studies the various levels of milk in the recording jars and asks, "Why is it that some cows produce so much more milk than others?"

"If I had the answer to that question, I'd be a wealthy man," Cooper says, explaining that there are lots of variables to milk production, including the age of the animal, her health, and her lactation stage.

"I just love that this"—Lucy gestures to her surroundings—"is called a dairy *parlor.*"

"It makes it sound like the kind of place where a proper young cow can sit down with a cold root beer and wait for gentlebull callers." Martha surveys the new lot of cows that have entered, noticing their snotty noses, muddy legs, and manure-smeared rumps. "Ladies," she calls out. "How about a little more attention to appearance and hygiene? You never know when a handsome bull might come a-callin'!"

Enchanted by Martha's silliness, Cooper laughs. "I'm afraid *I'm* the closest thing to a bull that any of these ladies get to see," he tells her.

"What about Pinckney?" Lucy asks. They'd driven by his pen on the way to the parlor. "I thought he was the bull for all the Tuckington cows."

"Actually, it's proven more cost-effective and reliable for me to inseminate the cows," Cooper says. "So these days, ole Pinckney only services the heifers."

Lucy and Martha exchange a look. *Services?*

"What exactly is the difference between a heifer and a cow, anyway?" Martha asks.

Cooper's eyes twinkle. "A heifer can't give milk. She's not a cow until she's freshened."

" 'Freshened'?"

"Until she's had a calf," he explains.

"I'm guessing a man came up with that euphemism," Lucy says. It takes a moment for her to realize that in the bovine world, she and Martha are still just a couple of heifers.

As if reading her mind, Martha says, "Always a heifer, never a cow."

EACH MORNING, the group returns to Cooper's house by 8 A.M. to the smell of freshly baked bread, the sound of bacon sizzling, and the sweet sight of Beatrice (clad in a black-and-white cow-patterned apron) scurrying around the kitchen scrambling and flipping and frying their breakfast. Large squares of softened butter, edges rounded by the heat of the kitchen, lie on the table and next to the stove.

On the first day, Bryce recoils when Beatrice hands him a plate piled high with scrambled eggs, home-cut slabs of bacon, fried potatoes, and buttered toast. "No offense, Beatrice," he says, looking at the portion, "but this meal has more calories than I usually consume in a week. Don't you have any Kashi or low-fat cottage cheese?"

Amen to that! Martha thinks, greatly relieved that someone else mentioned it before she had to. Why hadn't she thought to bring some nonfat yogurt?

Despite the girls' warnings in the car, Beatrice looks shocked: What kind of man turns down a proper breakfast? It only takes her a second, however, to decide what tack to take. She's a Southern woman after all, and flirtation is her currency. She turns up the volume on her accent and says, "I hope you're not suggesting that you're going to turn down a home-cooked meal, one that I made for you with my own two hands?" She tilts her head and gives him a look that is both tragic and seductive at once. "Besides, you must know that women love men with a little heft."

Walter perks up at this declaration and pats his spongy belly as if he'd created it with the pleasure of women in mind.

She said heft, not flab, thinks Lucy, reminded of a graffiti scribbled on a stall door in the ladies' room at La Luna: *Women will never be equal to men until they can walk down the street with a bald head and beer gut and still think they're beautiful.*

"The bigger you are, the safer we feel in your arms," Beatrice continues.

Martha looks to see if Lucy is as shocked by Beatrice's flirting as she is, but Lucy hasn't even noticed. She's stuck on Beatrice's comment about hefty men, remembering the first time she got undressed with Adam, horrified that her thighs were bigger than his. At the time, she wondered if she could ever feel secure dating a man who weighed only ten pounds more than her. Now, eyeing Adam's slender fingers, Lucy hands him the plate with the most bacon on it. "Eat up, sweetie," she tells him.

"I give you my word," Beatrice promises, tousling Bryce's hair. "My son will burn this breakfast off of you before lunchtime."

"If you say so," Bryce says, brushing his hair back into place.

If you're that gullible, thinks Martha, assessing the calorie, fat, and carbohydrate content of his plate, I should have just sold you a pill that'd turn you into the perfect man.

"How do *you* stay so svelte eating like this all the time?" Bryce asks.

Beatrice touches her waist, appreciative that a young man has noticed her figure. "Well, when you live in the country, you work for your food and that's pretty much all it takes. People aren't meant to sit at desks all day," she says, moving pans from the stove to the sink. "I tend to my vegetable garden and the chickens, and go dancing whenever I can."

Martha's eyes narrow. She knows there's a more plausible explanation for Beatrice's petiteness and does a quick plate count to discover that they're one shy. "Are you not having breakfast with us?" she asks innocently. *Don't make me find your Slim-Fast supply.*

Beatrice smiles. "Aren't you wicked for drawing attention to my bad manners," she says, and looks apologetically at the men. "I'm embarrassed to admit that I got so hungry making your breakfast, I couldn't wait."

"You never have to wait for us," Kurt says.

"Certainly not," Simon agrees. "You're a wonderful hostess."

"The best," Jesse says, perplexed by his sister's rudeness.

She's good, Martha thinks, marveling at the alacrity with which the men rush to her defense.

Beatrice shoots Martha a haughty look and resumes her conversation with Bryce. "Call me old-fashioned, but I think it's important to know where your food comes from," she says, with a touch of self-righteousness. "Look at your plate: the eggs are from my chickens; the pork from a farm down the road; the bread made fresh daily by our neighbors in exchange for butter we churn right here. Now, can you tell me where Kashi is from?"

Can you tell me where Tropicana orange juice comes from? thinks Martha, holding the carton up behind Beatrice.

Lucy frowns at her: *Put that down.*

SPRING IS A BUSY SEASON on the farm and dozens of jobs, big and small, need doing every day just to keep things on track: cows have to be milked, bred, and calved; land must be plowed, fertilized, and planted; fences require mending and equipment needs repair. Consequently, the campers' daily schedule at Tuckington Farm is rigorous and follows a predictable routine. The morning milking starts at sunrise and is followed by breakfast and whatever daily training session is scheduled (carpentry, machinery, and agriculture are all part of Man Camp's core curriculum). Then there's lunch, a much needed siesta, and the afternoon milking, which marks the end of the official workday and the beginning of whatever extracurricular activity Cooper has in store. Martha and Lucy take over the training operation at suppertime with informal lessons on manners, conversation, and chivalry. And, on nights when the campers are able to keep their eyes open, they show movies featuring strong male romantic leads.

—

Far and away the most grueling part of the campers' day is the training sessions organized by Cooper. Although he hadn't originally intended to work the men so hard, he also hadn't realized how dire the situation at Tuckington Farm would become—the foreclosure notice was a wake-up call. He knows he must take advantage of the six able-bodied men who are at his disposal. It might be his only chance to get the farm in shape before he has to sell off any land or machinery or livestock.

The first day's training session is in carpentry, and Cooper gives the campers the backbreaking task of replacing a stretch of wooden fence that starts in front of the house and meanders along the drive. Originally installed by his father forty years earlier, the job is long overdue. Using a hydraulic attachment on the front of a tractor, Cooper sets the new posts a few inches in front of the old, then shows the campers how to line up the planks properly.

"As you can see," he says, pointing to the weathered, old fence, "there're three horizontal boards—an upper, a middle, and a lower—each of which are twenty-one feet long. The posts are set at seven-foot intervals, which means that each board crosses three posts. Now, the trick to building a strong fence is stair-stepping the boards so that no two begin on the same post. Watch carefully!" He greases the point of a nail by running it through his hair and taps it lightly into the board to set it. Then, with two well-aimed, powerful strikes, he pounds it through to the post. "You want to hit the nail dead center."

Kurt flips his hammer up into the air and catches it on the way down. "Looks like a snap," he says, grabbing a board and getting to work right away.

Cooper smirks. Fence work is anything but a snap. He's done it for years (and has the Popeye forearms to show for it) and still dreads it like no other farm task. The other campers begin more cautiously, listening to Cooper's pointers.

The girls are sitting on nearby stumps, watching the action from a distance. Martha is entertained by Kurt's competitiveness and all of Bryce's bent nails, but Lucy worries that Adam might reinjure his back. Then Walter swaggers over, apparently preferring to talk about hard work rather than do it. He brags to the girls about his experiences on the Amish farm. "No plows or machines there. Only these," he says, slapping his soft biceps.

Lucy and Martha smile politely, but this only encourages Walter, who places both his hands down on top of the old fence, readying himself to leap over to their side to tell more stories.

Lucy jumps up to try to stop him—Cooper has just warned the campers that the old fence has electric wire running along the inside of the top board—but it's too late and midhurdle, Walter is zapped by a jolt of electricity powerful enough to keep a two-thousand-pound bull at bay. With a whimper, he crumples to the ground. Distracted by the commotion, Kurt smashes his thumb with the hammer. Two campers down.

Martha covers her eyes. "Remind me again how fence-building is relevant to their city lives?" she asks Lucy, suddenly worried about the men's safety.

"Everyone is okay," Lucy says in a calm voice as she assesses the damage. Already, Cooper has Walter on his feet and the two are laughing about the pain of getting shocked as if it's as basic a rite of passage to manhood as getting punched. And Kurt is fine, too, enjoying the opportunity to curse loudly.

Martha still can't look.

"Listen," Lucy reminds her, "you wanted to get them away from their cerebral New York lives and put them in touch with their physical selves."

"Right, right, right," Martha says, opening her eyes. "Building fences is manlier than counting widgets."

"Exactly. Now, it looks as if they need us. How about we pitch in and help?"

"Good idea," Martha says, getting up.

But Cooper vetoes their plan. "What if you're better at it than them?"

The next day's training session is on engine maintenance and repair, and is held in the machine shop, a long, low cinder-block building that smells of oil. It has a tin roof and windows that are opaque with dirt, making the inside dark and cool. Worktables covered with greasy tools line one wall. Gears, acetylene torches, lengths of chain, and pieces of long-dead machinery lie scattered about the floor. Outside, six farm vehicles await the campers' attention.

Cooper walks the men through several simple maintenance routines like checking fluids (steering, transmission, and wiper), changing oil and oil filters, and flushing out radiators, as well as quick fixes such as jump- and roll-starts, and what to do if a vehicle overheats. Then he sets the campers to work lubing the long-neglected vehicles parked out front.

"How adorable," Lucy says, sitting next to Martha on the grass. "Look at the schmutz on Adam's forehead. And your brother's holding a grease gun!"

Martha doesn't reply. She's thinking about Cooper and how differently she thought their week together would be. She'd imagined stolen kisses behind cowsheds, secret walks in the woods, and clandestine trips into town. The reality is there's been zero romance. "Lucy, do you think there's anything going on between Cooper and this Jolene Beatrice keeps talking about?"

"No way," Lucy says. "Cooper would never have encouraged you if he had a girlfriend."

EACH AFTERNOON, when the day's work is done and while the women are preparing dinner, Cooper takes the campers out for an all-male adventure, an extracurricular activity that he hopes will uncover long-buried masculine inclinations in them. The first day, he teaches them how to shoot his father's favorite rifle, a Marlin .22, at a large sinkhole on the property. He brings plenty of ammo and shows them how to line up a target in the sight's notch, letting them in on the secret to a steady shot: "You want to take a deep breath, let it out entirely, then gradually tighten your finger on the trigger." He demonstrates as he says this, aiming at a milkweed pod, which he hits dead center, creating a poof of white feathers that drift away on the breeze.

One by one the men get up to shoot, thrilled by the noise and the kick of the gun. Though they aren't great marksmen, they are enthusiastic and this encourages Cooper to suggest they all try groundhog-hunting some evening.

Kurt responds with a loud, "Huah," as if he'd just been ordered to storm the beaches at Normandy.

Prompted by Kurt's reaction, Cooper continues: "You have to stalk them, see, by imitating their whistle." He makes a shrill *wheep-wheep-wheep* sound. "Then, when one of them pops his fuzzy head up out of his hole, BLAM!" he shouts, mock-firing his rifle. "But they have really thick hides and tons of subcutaneous fat—think little bears—so you usually have to nail them again up close."

Jesse's face contorts. He recently edited a book called *Forest Friends,* about a chipmunk and woodchuck who team up when a forest fire threatens their homes. He's pretty sure that groundhogs are relatives.

Cooper realizes he's gone overboard and adds a defensive: "Their holes are a real menace to the cows."

Figuring that he'll slowly warm them up to the idea of killing, the next evening Cooper takes them to his father's favorite fishing spot on the swollen Manasseh River. It's a place so familiar to him that he knows the outline of the branches against the sky, how the light will fall, and where the shadows will land. He lines the men up on the river's edge and shows them how to cast, placing his lure near a rocky outcropping in the middle of the river. Within seconds, a trout strikes, and Cooper effortlessly pulls it to shore.

Bryce squats down to study the fish up close. "It looks exactly like the ones at the *pêcherie* near my apartment," he says, surprised.

"Not quite yet," Cooper remarks, flicking open his pocketknife and inserting the tip forcefully in between the pectoral fins of the still-flopping fish, "but it will in about one second." With one swift gesture, he slices down the length of the body and guts the trout, tossing a small fistful of intestines into the river. "One down, nine to go for supper."

Disgusted, Jesse tries to warn the trout by splashing by the river's edge, but it does little to save them from Cooper, who seems to hook one with almost every cast.

Simon and Kurt are the only campers who actually catch fish, one apiece. The rest of the men, exhausted from the day's physical labor, are content to enjoy the repetitive motion of casting and the rare opportunity to relax their eyes on a landscape devoid of steel or pavement or neon.

MIDWAY THROUGH THE WEEK, Cooper announces that he'll be inseminating cows after breakfast and gives the men the option of joining him in lieu of helping his farmhands plant the spring wheat crop. When there are no takers, Martha senses opportunity and volunteers. It sounds more fun than watching the campers drive bulldozers, and she's eager for time alone with Cooper.

The day is sunny but not warm, and Martha wraps her cardigan tightly around herself, hooking an arm through Cooper's as they walk to the barn.

He steers her across the pasture, avoiding the driveway in case the foreclosure notice he took down that first night has been replaced already. His mind is busy with worry about the farm: Should he sell off one hundred acres to that developer who's been making offers for the last year? Should he auction off part of the herd? Either solution would make his father turn in his grave. How could he have let things get this bad? He manages to make small talk with Martha, relaying cow facts that he could recite in his sleep, but his mind is elsewhere. "It's all about timing," he says when she asks about insemination. "Estrus only lasts about eight hours, so when you see the signs, you have to move quickly."

"And what are the signs?" she asks suggestively, delighted to steer the conversation toward mating.

"The cows start mounting each other," Cooper says, oblivious to Martha's flirting, and continues his clinical explanation of bovine reproduction. When they enter the Cow Palace, he takes her straight to the liquid-nitrogen tank where he stores his supply of bull semen. He opens the tank, reaches through the curlicues of smoke, and plucks out a slim straw of ejaculate, which he places in a mug filled with lukewarm water. When it reaches the correct temperature, he snips off one end and threads the straw inside a stainless steel insemination gun. Then he guides Martha to where the cows are waiting, their heads locked between bars to keep them from moving. There, he pulls on a long plastic glove, dabs some mineral oil onto the fingertips, and pushes the cow's tail aside.

Martha races up to the cow's head before Cooper inserts his hand. "If it's all the same to you," she whispers to the cow, #42 according to its ear tag, "I'd like to call you Bessie." She strokes Bessie's black-and-white head and admires her long eyelashes. "You sure are one beautiful cow," Martha says, "and I think he *really* likes you. Yep, he's definitely going to call."

"What are you telling number forty two?" Cooper asks, now holding the cow's uterus through the walls of her rectum, threading the insemination gun into her vagina, where he releases the sperm.

"Just some pillow talk," Martha answers, noticing that Bessie seems rather indifferent to what's going on. "A girl needs to be reassured of her man's affection every once in a while," she says, pleased by her own directness.

"Done," says Cooper, withdrawing his arm. "Well, number forty-two should feel reassured that two thousand pounds of bull isn't pounding on her. Isn't that right, cow?"

Martha sighs, embarrassed that Cooper didn't even pick up on what she said.

Patting the cow's rump, Cooper says a gentle, "Get pregnant, cow."

For a moment, Martha melts at how sweet his voice sounds. "Who's the daddy, anyway?" she asks.

After peeling off the used glove and tossing it into the garbage, Cooper hands Martha the March issue of *Holstein Director,* which has been folded into his back pocket.

Martha's eyes widen. The magazine, subtitled *Select Sires,* is full of personal ads, not for loveless singles, but for bulls whose appeal is based on their ability to produce superior milking cows. Enticing photographs of their offspring fill the pages, along with detailed descriptions of udders, teats, and rumps. "I just can't believe this," she says, opening up to a *Playboy*-style center-fold of Sunshine, daughter of Otto the bull. The photo of Sunshine is taken in three-quarter profile from the rear, highlighting her ample bag and lean body. "I wonder what her hobbies are!" Martha says, imagining: *Expert at fly-swatting with tail, can moo "Old Man River," makes heart-shaped cow paddies.*

"Hey, I use Otto quite a bit," Cooper says, sounding slightly defensive.

Why aren't you looking at me the way you did in New York? Martha wants to scream, but continues to discuss the magazine. "Well then, you know all about his excellent genetics: 'square-placed udders and superior overall dairyness.' "

"Indeed I do," Cooper says. "He's father to seventy-five percent of the Tuckington cows and affordable to boot."

It takes Martha a moment to process this information, which

means that Otto has impregnated mothers and daughters, sisters, aunts, and cousins. *Yuck.*

Cooper registers Martha's expression of disgust. "Look on the bright side," he tells her, "this is the very concept you wish to impart to the campers: make yourselves indispensable to women or risk becoming obsolete." He walks her back toward the nitrogen tank. "Can you think of a more humbling place to be a man than on a dairy farm?" he asks. "One bull is all any farmer has ever needed to meet the reproductive requirements of all of his cows." He grabs another straw of Otto's semen and holds it up to make his point. "And now, even that bull isn't strictly necessary."

Martha touches Cooper's arm, trying to think of a way to bring the conversation around to what's going on between them. What comes out of her mouth is: "I'm not sure your mother likes me very much."

Cooper shakes his head dismissively and says, "That's just Mom." As he waits for a second batch of semen to warm to room temperature, his mind drifts back once again to the foreclosure notice and he starts to frown.

Just ask him what's going on, Martha thinks, trying to read meaning into his furrowed brow. She hears herself say, "She keeps mentioning a friend of yours named Jolene."

But Cooper is a million miles away, negotiating with bankers, pleading for more time, signing over deeds to the auctioneer. When he looks back at Martha a moment later, he realizes he hasn't heard a word she's said. He stares at her, feeling idiotic. She's beautiful with the morning light streaming onto her hair and he can't imagine how he's been able to think of anything else. In the time it takes him to decide to tell her that, she's turned to leave the barn.

CHAPTER 10

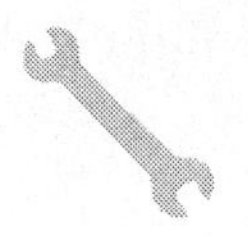

"I'm not denyin' the women are foolish: God almighty made 'em to match the men."

George Eliot

IT'S AFTER DINNER and the campers are watching *An Officer and a Gentleman,* one of dozens of videos that Martha brought with her to the farm, the objective being to expose the men to as wide an array of positive masculine styles as possible. The films feature stars like Sam Shepard, Humphrey Bogart, and Sean Connery in roles where their masculinity is somehow put to the test. In some the hero gets the girl, in others he doesn't, but always he is courageous and gallant under fire, at his core a gentleman.

The campers are strewn about the living room like rag dolls: splayed out on the floor, flopped over chairs, stretched across sofas. Exhausted from another day of hard work and full of Beatrice's fried-chicken supper, the men are content to absorb lessons on manliness by osmosis, half asleep as they watch the movie.

At a pivotal moment in the film—right after Zack Mayo's best friend commits suicide and transforms Zack from a self-absorbed hotshot into a team player and leader—Martha taps Lucy's shoulder and points to the door. She needs to talk.

Lucy hopes that whatever is bothering Martha can wait until after Richard Gere carries Debra Winger out of the factory, but her friend looks insistent. Lucy disentangles herself from Adam. "I have to go," she whispers into his ear. "Could you lead the postfilm discussion on Zack Mayo's transformation?"

Adam responds in a look: *Not a chance.*

Lucy and Martha leave the living room mostly unnoticed and slip out the back door, where they make their way to the far end of the yard and lean their backs against the broad trunk of a majestic silver maple tree. The night sky is clear and jam-packed with stars, and a nearly full moon hovers low above the hills.

"God, isn't spring amazing? May is such a sexy month," Lucy says over a commotion of peepers in a nearby pond. "Just listen to all that courtship." She wishes Adam were outside, too.

"Yes," Martha says sourly, "romance is in the air."

"Did you know that peepers can repeat their calls over four thousand times a night?" It's courtship facts like these, which Lucy knows by the hundreds, that can make her dismayed by Adam's lack of romantic effort. When was the last time he sang to her?

Martha groans. "Exactly what is it about their clamor that attracts females? I can barely sleep through all the racket."

Lucy smiles at her friend's bah-humbug attitude. "Well, at the very least, you have to admit that it's kind of amazing how our brains deal with unfamiliar sounds. Just think about it: you can sleep through ambulances screaming down Ninth Avenue at four A.M., but a little frog singing a love song keeps you up."

Martha rolls her eyes. "Forgive me if I'm not in the mood to marvel at the wonders of nature tonight."

"I'm sorry," Lucy says. "What's going on?"

Martha doesn't quite know where to begin. "I'm just not cut out for farm living. The hours are nuts and I'm sick of cooking and cleaning and being on the sidelines. Look at me, I've been here, what, four days? And I'm a total wreck. I'm not sleeping well. I've got enough cuts and bruises to land a part as a battered woman. And I'm this close," she says, pinching her thumb and forefinger together, "to setting up an emergency phoner with my shrink to discuss that bitch Beatrice. Exactly what have I done to deserve her treatment?"

"Nothing." Lucy puts an arm around her friend. "She's just being possessive of her only son. Now that her husband's gone, Cooper's all she has left. Who can blame her?"

I can, thinks Martha, who has always found Lucy's ability to empathize with the wrong party annoying. She pulls blades of grass out of the ground one at a time. "Things aren't going well with Cooper," she says softly. "They just aren't going, period."

"Have you tried talking to him?"

"I tried to when we were inseminating cows, but everything came out wrong. Instead of asking what was up between us, I criticized his mother and grilled him about Jolene."

"I'm sure it didn't go as badly as you think," Lucy says, shifting to lie on her back and look up at the sky, where she finds the Big Dipper tipped at a precarious angle, looking as if it might slosh its contents all over the galaxy. "Give him the benefit of the doubt. I think Cooper has something on his mind and you just need to be patient." Lucy knows patience has never been Martha's strong suit.

A moment passes and they hear the screen door creak open and snap shut. Cooper and Adam are standing on the back porch, gazing out over the lawn.

"We're down here," Lucy calls out, waving.

Adam seems tall standing next to Cooper, which pleases Lucy, who's noticed that her boyfriend has been looking especially handsome, and attributes it to all the outdoor work. His normally stooped shoulders are square and high, and his pasty winter complexion has taken on a light bronze sheen. "You have to admit, it's kind of ironic that we're the ones having a hard time adjusting to life at Man Camp." She laughs. "The men seem to be thriving while we're locked in the kitchen."

"Yeah. It's fucking hilarious," Martha says.

"Come on. A little poetic justice is only fair."

"I guess I don't care about fair."

Cooper and Adam amble across the lawn, stopping in front of them.

"Would you look at all those stars," Adam says, letting out a low whistle.

"Not a sight you get to see much of in the big city, huh, Martha?" says Cooper, looking up at the sky.

Martha thinks about the sights she hasn't gotten to see much of in the country: watercress, newspapers with international coverage, naked men.

"To me," he goes on dreamily, "stars are just about proof positive of God's existence."

"How's that?" Lucy asks.

"You know, they're just totally unnecessary miracles spattered across the sky to remind us that He's here to help if we get lost," Cooper answers, studying the three-starred dagger that hangs from Orion's belt.

A crescendo of croaking fills the silence that follows.

"Back in the big city, we call that a 'conversation stopper,' " Adam says.

Cooper laughs, and then Lucy does, too, relieved that Adam's joke has gone over well, pleased that the two of them are getting along.

"Well, I just came out to say good night," Cooper says. "I'm dog tired from the day's work." He taps the toe of his boot against Martha's shoe. "Thanks for the help with the cows this morning."

"No problem. Good night," Martha says, guessing it must be all of nine-thirty. She watches Cooper's back get small as he walks toward the house. "Sweet dreams," she adds quietly as the screen door springs closed behind him. She waits a few minutes before getting up and brushing the twigs and grass off the back of her pants. "I need to go check on my charges," she says, taking a step toward the house. Then she hesitates. "Adam, do you think the men are having a good time?"

"Amazingly enough, I really do. They're working their asses off, but they're loving it, and I actually think they're learning things, too," he says, speaking from the perspective of the teacher he thinks he is. "Well, perhaps not Bryce. That guy's too far gone, but three out of four isn't bad."

Or five out of six, thinks Martha, including Jesse and Adam in her private tally.

"There's something about this place that gets you out of your head," Adam continues. "Could just be the hard work and fresh air, but even *I'm* experiencing it. For the first time in forever, I haven't been obsessing about my dissertation and yet somehow, subconsciously, I guess, I'm working through things." He looks down at Lucy. "I've figured out the ending."

"Are you serious?" Lucy says, propping herself up on her elbows.

Adam drops to his knees, explaining that he's decided to use farming as the third business model for his dissertation, which perfectly illustrates his theory on procrastination.

Upon hearing phrases like behavioral predictiveness, procedural rationality, and economic anomalies, Martha says a sarcastic, "Fascinating," and bids them a final good night.

Lucy takes Adam's hand and pulls him the rest of the way to the ground. "I can't believe you're unstuck."

"Well, believe it. The end's in sight." He rolls onto his back and pulls her on top of him. "And you know who I have to thank for that? You, for being so patient with me this last year. You, for dragging me along as an adjunct professor on this crazy vacation. You, for just being you." He kisses her. "You know what the only problem with this place is? We don't get enough time together."

"I'm so happy you like it here," Lucy says, relishing the effects Adam's words have on her guilty conscience. "I had my doubts you'd like it here, you know." She props herself up on his chest and looks into his dark eyes. "And don't you just adore Cooper now that you've gotten to know him better?"

"He's a good guy."

Lucy hears a *but* in Adam's voice and asks him what it is.

He hesitates. "*But* . . . doesn't any part of the scientist in you get wigged out by all his God stuff?"

The truth is Cooper's outspoken religiousness has always wigged Lucy out, even as a college student, and yet now she feels the need to defend her old friend. "Jesus, Adam, it's religion, not witchcraft."

Adam's look says, *What's the difference?*

"Don't be so narrow-minded. Historically, lots of great scientists were religious. Like Darwin," Lucy says, wishing she could come up with someone more contemporary.

"Okay, let's drop it," Adam says, feeling Lucy's mood shift away from romance. "Let's take a walk," he proposes, pulling her to her feet. Taking her hand in his, he guides her out the gate and along the fence, past pasture after pasture, some full of cows, the moon rising and brightening their way.

When they come to a bend where the road dips, Lucy sees a small cluster of crocuses and snatches one. "There's something about being around natural beauty that changes my outlook on life," she says, handing him the flower.

"A biologist I know once told me that a flower is a plant's way of making love."

"I can't believe you remember that." Lucy circles her arms around his neck.

"I remember everything you tell me," Adam says, gently backing her up against a nearby birch tree where he starts to kiss her.

Lucy returns the kiss and closes her eyes. She places her palms on the tree's papery bark and reads hope into a row of raised bumps that feel like braille letters.

Adam's fingers start to work the buttons of her blouse and Lucy's knees soften. He pulls her shirt open and runs his hands along the intersection of her belly and belt, feeling the muscles contract beneath his touch. Then he steps back to take off his own shirt when an eerie *who-ah-whoo* causes Lucy's eyes to snap open.

"What was that?"

Adam pulls her close to him. "Don't worry, Luce," he says, resting his chin on her head. "It's just a great horned owl." The men had heard the same call a few mornings ago and Cooper told them that these owls are all over the Manasseh Valley.

Lucy relaxes into Adam's arms and he spreads his shirt on the ground, lowering her on top of it and lying beside her on the grass.

INSIDE THE HOUSE, Martha checks on the campers. Jesse, Simon, and Walter have already gone to bed, leaving only Kurt and Bryce to discuss the movie.

"So, what did you think?" she asks.

Kurt gives her a thumbs-down. "Too schmaltzy," he says. "Though Louis Gossett, Junior kicked ass as the gunnery sergeant."

Bryce looks at his hands, apparently unhappy with manual labor's effect on them. "The uniforms were awesome."

It's then Martha realizes Adam is right: Man Camp will have no effect on Bryce. Bryce is who he is, and who he is, is a man who likes to make sweaters for his dog, watch chick flicks, and talk about celebrity hook-ups. He will always be more comfortable shopping than fence-building. Though he was a sport to come to Tuckington Farm, Martha realizes that in his heart, he's not interested in becoming more masculine, only in getting more women. And why should the two be mutually exclusive? After all, you don't need to know how to chop wood or hunt in New York City and, if you can afford a car, you can afford to have someone else change the oil. She remembers her father's preppy friends in the suburbs, men who wore pink sweaters and seersucker pants and still managed to find wives and happiness. Perhaps metrosexuals are just our generation's more fashionable version of them, she thinks.

Though she's not particularly tired, Martha wants to be alone and excuses herself to go to bed. She walks up the stairs, surprised to find Cooper waiting on the love seat at the top of the landing. He motions for her to sit beside him and takes her hand. "I want to apologize for being so distracted the last few days."

The words trigger flutters in Martha's stomach. She looks at Cooper and sees a man who is sorry, *very* sorry. She sits quietly, waiting for him to elaborate, but instead he kisses her in such a way that she forgets an explanation is in order. Before she knows it, Cooper is tossing pillows onto the floor and they're reclining on the tiny sofa, their bodies moving against each other.

Suddenly, Beatrice's voice calls up from downstairs, "I hope you're not making a mess up there! Ruth just cleaned today." She flicks on the light from below and hums her way up the stairs.

Martha and Cooper sit up. Martha straightens her clothes and checks her hair, feeling as if she's back in junior high.

Beatrice arrives with a feather duster in hand. "Ruth always forgets to do these bookshelves," she says, occupying herself with the task.

Cooper gives a resigned exhale.

Do something! Martha thinks, and starts to count to three. She stops at one, too furious to go on. Abruptly standing up, she says good night and walks toward her room, at the opposite end of the hallway from Cooper's. It occurs to Martha as she closes the door that Beatrice never retires until she's safely tucked away in the tiny guest bedroom.

Martha flops down on the bed, buries her face in the pillow, and groans. She picks up a book to distract herself, tries to read, and puts it down. A few minutes later, she picks it up again. A moth is trapped in the shade of her reading lamp, its wings thudding against the sides. She snaps her book shut, pulls the covers up to her chin, and turns off the light. Out the window she sees the barn, tiny in the distance, and wonders if the cows are asleep. Then she wonders if the men have gone to bed, if she's put on weight, if Beatrice has always been this interfering, and if, indeed, stars are totally unnecessary miracles. Her mind flits from subject to subject until it lands on what's bothering her: *What has been distracting Cooper?* But the more she tries to focus on the problem, the blurrier it gets until, at last, sleep consumes her.

THE NEXT DAY, Cooper supervises the morning milking and then leaves for town, where he has an appointment at the local bank. He instructs the men to meet his farmhand, Roy Snedegar, at the south pasture after breakfast to clear the land, which has gone to seed. He promises to be back in time for lunch and to take them to the pistol range for some afternoon target practice.

The weather is beautiful and the men decide to walk to the field rather than drive, and set out along the dirt road leading from the farmhouse to the main road. They pass the fence they built, a field they planted, and a number of newly tuned-up farm vehicles. Aware that their time at Tuckington Farm is more than half over, the men are feeling especially tolerant of one another, and no one even minds when Simon gives a mini-lecture on the benefits of crop rotation. Adam is whistling. With his dissertation neatly falling into place in his head, he's ready for another day of work.

As they round the final bend leading to the south pasture, they see a sheriff's car pull out of Tuckington Drive and onto the main road. An orange sign is tacked to the post.

"What is that?" Bryce asks.

"Holy shit," Adam says, reading the small print. " 'Upon breach of the condition of mortgage by nonpayment or non-performance of the condition stipulated in such mortgage . . . ' My God, it's a foreclosure notice. Cooper's about to lose Tuckington Farm." He skims the rest of the notice, reading certain words and phrases aloud: " 'Public taking.' 'Final determination.' 'Petition to vacate.' "

"I guess Mr. Perfect Alpha Male doesn't have everything so under control after all," Kurt says.

BACK AT THE FARMHOUSE, the women clear the breakfast dishes and put the finishing touches on Operation Damsels in Distress. Lucy tells Martha about the cave system where they plan to get "lost" later. "Tuckington Farm sits on what's known as a karst area, essentially a foundation of water-soluble limestone," she says, thinking more information will make Martha more enthusiastic about their impending adventure, though she knows enough not to mention that albino cave spiders inhabit them. "Let's synchronize our watches."

"I love your sense of daring, Lucy," Beatrice says.

Getting away from you is worth a few hours in a clammy cave, thinks Martha, accidentally banging her hip against the corner of the kitchen island and acquiring yet another bruise.

"Cooper once told me the saddest story about his favorite calf getting lost in there," Lucy says, turning to Martha. "He was only eight years old, and he and his father searched all morning for the calf, following the sounds of its bawling. But it kept walking away from them and further into the cave, until at some point, his dad decided that enough was enough and said, 'Good luck, calf,' and dragged Cooper out."

"Then the *real* bawling began," Beatrice takes over. "The boy was inconsolable!" She looks at the kitchen clock. "It's exactly eleven."

Lucy adjusts her watch. "Okay. So, we go in the main entrance, take a right at the far end of the first big chamber, walk in about fifty yards, and sit on the flat rock and wait," she says, repeating their plan. "When the campers come back for lunch at noon, you act alarmed, tell them Martha and I have been missing for hours, and they come save us. Instant heroes."

"Perfect."

"And Cooper is our back-up plan, in case anything goes wrong," Lucy adds.

"Where is Cooper?" asks Martha, who overslept this morning and hasn't seen him since their ill-fated make-out session the night before.

"If there is one thing you should know about me, I never intrude into my son's personal life," Beatrice replies, taking a dainty sip of coffee. "Sometimes his engagements in town last well into the night." Her voice is thick with innuendo.

Martha reminds herself that "well into the night" in the Tuckington household probably means 8 P.M., and wills herself not to let Beatrice get to her.

"Cooper is supposed to be back by lunch," Lucy assures her. "If for any reason the campers can't find us, Cooper definitely will."

"Let's hope he does a better job with us than he did with his calf," Martha says under her breath. "Now, shall we get this show on the road?"

"Before you two leave, we should discuss the party," Beatrice says. "We've invited fifty neighbors and friends to come over on Friday and we haven't even planned the menu!"

"How about starting with a huge salad," suggests Martha,

longing for the taste of bitter greens. She pictures a collage of arugula, avocados, and cherry tomatoes in an enormous wooden bowl.

"Not a bad idea," Beatrice says, sounding surprised. "Jolene's potato salad won first prize at the Neola County fair last year. I bet she'd whip us up a batch. Cooper just loves her cooking."

Potato salad is *not* salad, thinks Martha, but says, "Sounds delish."

"I was thinking about ribs as the entrée," Beatrice says.

The phone rings and when Beatrice goes to answer it, Martha puts on her jean jacket and says, "Now, Luce. We're leaving *now.*"

As they walk across the property to the cave entrance at the bottom of the sinkhole, Martha tries to imagine the vast limestone underworld that Lucy has described, full of secret tunnels and rooms. "What keeps the houses from tumbling in?" she wonders aloud. "If you ask me, it doesn't sound too safe to live above a network of caves."

"Don't be ridiculous," Lucy says.

But when they arrive at the sinkhole, a hundred-foot-long basin where the earth has collapsed in on itself and formed a crater large enough to swallow a house, Martha's fears seem plausible. Its sloping sides are covered in West Virginia creeper, which they have to push aside to climb down to the cave's rocky entrance. The passageway is barely wide enough to squeeze through.

"Have we discussed my claustrophobia of late?" Martha asks, flicking on their flashlight.

"Not applicable to caves *at all,*" Lucy responds, entering

first. "Your brand of claustrophobia is more about people than space. It's the whole packed elevator/crowded train thing, and has less to do with the walls closing in than with the fear that you'll be trapped with strangers who'll bore you to death."

"Oh yeah," Martha says and drops the subject. She looks at her watch. "No more than an hour, right?"

"An hour, tops."

They wander along single file. The entrance channel is narrow and dark and damp, with several tiny rooms branching off of it.

"This kind of reminds me of my first apartment in New York," Martha says. "Only it's bigger and has better light."

Lucy laughs. "And fewer bugs!"

"Bugs live in caves?"

"Um . . ."

"What about bats?"

Lucy hears genuine panic rising in Martha's voice and tries to calm her. "Bats have a bad rap. They hardly ever bite, and all that vampire stuff is nonsense."

The passageway snakes around a bend and then opens up into a huge room, as large as a subway tunnel, with shiny dark walls, slick with water.

"This must be the big chamber."

"Wow. It's incredible," Martha says, touching the slippery walls. She turns her flashlight on and off, amazed at how black this black really is. "Does it just go on like this for miles?"

"I think so."

"Oh, look at that weird formation," Martha says, pointing to a stalagmite at the far end of the cavern. They go over to examine it and walk into another passageway that leads them past several smaller rooms and into an even larger chamber.

"Hold up," Lucy says. "I'm glad to see you getting into the

spirit of things, but this damsel wants to find the meeting spot." They start walking back the way they came, but are startled to discover that every passageway looks the same. Almost immediately, they come to a branch they don't recall. They pick a direction and pass several other unfamiliar branches. Soon they're so turned around that they're not sure if they're headed out or farther in, or simply going in circles.

Lucy notices lots of bones and teeth on the rocks, which lend a creepy, mortuary feel to the place and makes her think of Cooper's calf. A slightly opaque, brown salamander skitters across a rock and she recalls Cooper once telling her that cave inhabitants become more translucent the farther in they live. Based on that fact, Lucy figures they mustn't be too lost, *yet,* but there are miles and miles of caves in the area. "How about we sit tight. The men will come looking as soon as Beatrice tells them we're missing."

"Good idea," Martha says, feeling more stupid than scared. *Really* getting lost wasn't part of the plan. She's sure Jolene doesn't do dumb shit like this.

THE CAMPERS SPEND the morning reclaiming the south pasture, which is overgrown with weeds and wildflowers and small trees. Under the dour direction of Roy Snedegar, a quiet, skinny man in overalls, the men take turns using the farm's small bulldozer to push over saplings, and the bush hog (a lawn mower on steroids) to chew up light brush and shrubs. Adam loads the debris onto a hay wagon and hauls it to a pit where it will be burned. The men who aren't operating the big machines use chain saws and shovels to remove stumps. By lunchtime, all the campers are ready to quit work except Kurt, who is digging out a stubborn root. "Just let me finish this last one," he says, wiping his arm across his forehead and leaving a brown smear on his skin.

By the time they return to the farmhouse, they're almost an hour late and Beatrice is genuinely alarmed, pacing back and forth on the porch with Tor and Tap at her side. She tells the campers that the girls never returned from their spelunking expedition and she hasn't been able to reach Cooper. She has flashlights lined up in a row on the railing and a bag of red poker chips to use as trail markers.

With the exception of Jesse and Adam, who are sick with worry, the campers are excited at the prospect of saving Lucy and Martha. Without much debate, they make a plan: Kurt assumes authority and sets up a command center in the farmhouse to coordinate information from the field. Adam and Jesse form the primary rescue team and leave with the equipment and dogs, agreeing to return in one hour for a debriefing. Simon and Walter drive into Neola to search for Cooper.

Bryce helps Beatrice with lunch.

MARTHA AND LUCY have been sitting on their rock long enough to sing every Beatles song they can remember, when Lucy notices that their flashlight is dimming. "We better turn that out for a while."

Martha clicks off the light and it is darker than any darkness either of them has ever experienced.

"Here comes the sun, do-da-do-da," Lucy sings, expecting Martha to laugh, but all she hears is water trickling down the cave walls.

"As long as we're going to die together," Martha says, "is there anything you feel like you should tell me?"

"Huh?"

"Like some secret or completely humiliating moment that you thought you'd gotten away with?"

"I don't think so," Lucy says.

"Come on, I'll tell you one if you tell me one. I'll even go first."

"Fair enough," Lucy says, hoping that Martha's story will buy her enough time to come up with one of her own.

Martha begins: "Remember that time we got massages at De-Stress last winter?"

"Yes."

"And remember how blissed out I was in the steam room afterwards?"

"Yes."

"Well, it was because—" Martha stops midsentence and giggles. "It was because the guy massaged my breasts."

"Are you kidding? That's disgusting! What did you do?"

"What did I do?"

"I mean, did you report him or call the police?"

"Um, not really," Martha says, giggling some more. "It wasn't exactly one-way. I like to think that the music and candles had something to do with it."

"Jesus, Martha."

"Is that really the best response you can come up with?"

"Did you tip him?"

Martha nods in the darkness. "Big-time."

"That's practically prostitution."

"Um, Luce," Martha says. "Here's the big rule in terms of revelation: you're not allowed to judge the person. Now, your turn."

Lucy takes a deep breath of the clammy air, wondering why the temperature in caves is a constant fifty-three degrees. A secret, she thinks. Something embarrassing. Nothing pops immediately to mind. "I once hugged a bunny to death?" she says, phrasing it more as a question than a statement.

"You *what*?"

"I hugged a bunny to death. At least I think I did. It was back in kindergarten. I hugged it and hugged it, then it went limp. Next think I knew, Miss Atmore came over and took Fluffy away."

"Luce?"

"Yes?"

"You do understand that these two stories are not remotely alike, right? Mine is about humiliation. Yours is about . . . well, I'm not even sure what yours is about."

Lucy struggles to think of a better story.

"Luce?"

"Yes?"

"I'm really scared."

"I am, too, but we're going to be fine," Lucy assures her. "We have plenty of water and can survive without food for a week. Besides, by now the men must know we're missing and are looking for us."

"We *think* they know we're missing. What if Beatrice never told them?"

"Don't be ridiculous. Besides, Cooper knows."

Martha hears a sound. "What was that?"

They both listen hopefully. Nothing.

Martha shrieks. "I just felt something slither against my leg."

"Calm down. It was probably just a salamander."

"A salamander is *not* okay," Martha says. She's quiet for a moment. "I'll call my mother every day. I'll quit smoking. I'll go to church. I'll stop—"

"What on earth are you doing?" Lucy says.

"Praying," Martha says. "It's something we lapsed Catholics do in a pinch."

Lucy hears a noise in the distance and shushes Martha. The muffled sound of dogs barking deep in the caves echoes softly in their chamber. "I bet it's them! We're here!" Lucy shouts. "We're over here." She grabs the flashlight and turns it on.

Within moments, Tor and Tap are splashing toward them, wagging their tails.

"Good boys," Martha says, stroking their heads. "You are such good, good boys."

Soon after, they hear the sloshing of larger animals, and Adam and Jesse pop their heads out of a tunnel, aiming bright spotlights at them. Adam rushes over to Lucy and takes her in his arms. "Baby, I was so worried about you."

Lucy burrows her face into his neck.

"You're a real hero, larvae," Martha says, hugging her brother. "Who would have guessed that you'd go into a cave for me? Thank you." She looks around to see if Cooper is part of the rescue party.

He's not.

—

On the walk back to the farmhouse, Adam tells Lucy about the foreclosure sign. They are walking hand in hand, several paces ahead of Martha and Jesse. "Some serious shit's going on," he says. "I don't know what, but I think it's safe to say Cooper's in trouble."

Why didn't Cooper tell me? Lucy wonders. She looks over her shoulder at Martha, who's walking beside her brother and looking at the ground. This is why Cooper has been distant around you, Lucy realizes. She hangs back, hooks arms with her despondent friend, and pulls her aside. "I've found out what the problem is," Lucy says, repeating to Martha what Adam has just told her. "It must be what's been distracting Cooper. I bet it's why he's at the bank right now."

Martha looks at her blankly.

"Don't you get it?" Lucy says. "Your weaverbird can't pursue you until his nest is in order."

CHAPTER 11

"The true measure of a man is how he treats someone who can do him absolutely no good."

Ann Landers

"SHAME ON YOU TWO for worrying everyone like that!" Beatrice scolds, winking slyly at Lucy and Martha when they return from the caves.

It's past two-thirty when the group finally sits down to eat lunch and devours the ham and cheese sandwiches that Beatrice and Bryce prepared. The men are preoccupied with the farm's predicament, but unable to speak openly about it in front of Beatrice. They sit in silence wondering what, if anything, they can do to help. The women are also subdued, embarrassed at needing to be rescued for real. Cooper is delayed at the bank, but calls to arrange for the campers to meet him at the Sleepy Creek Pistol Range in an hour for the target practice he promised.

"Chop, chop, ladies," Beatrice says when the group is finished eating. "Let's clear this table and get to work on our party."

Martha bristles at the word *our,* and starts collecting dishes. She glares at the men, who make no move to help. At home, any one of them would get up, but here it's as if it doesn't occur to them, not even to her extremely well-trained brother.

"And gentlemen," Beatrice says in a singsongy voice, "I have a little surprise for you. Tomorrow, I'm going to teach you how to two-step." She gives a quick demonstration, gracefully two-stepping halfway around the table to a full stop behind Bryce's chair. "In my opinion, there's nothing more appealing than a man who knows how to dance." She places her hands on Bryce's shoulders. "But I'm warning you, once you get a taste for Southern belles, you'll never go back to those Yankees again."

Some silverware tumbles off the plate Martha's carrying and clatters to the floor.

Beatrice smiles as if just realizing her faux pas and adds, "Present company excluded, of course."

THE SLEEPY CREEK PISTOL RANGE is at the northernmost edge of the Manasseh Valley, a good twenty miles from Tuckington Farm, and the drive gives the campers time to talk and plan. They've had all day to chew on the meaning of bank meetings and foreclosure notices and now they're eager to dust off their arsenal of high-tech gadgets—laptops, GPS devices, HP calculators, Blackberries, and Palm Pilots—and help. They'll show Cooper that city boys know a thing or two.

"Let's start with what we know," Adam says, surveying the truck's occupants. "We have a businessman, a news producer, a historian, an advertising executive, and"—he pauses for a moment when his eyes land on Jesse—"a children's book editor. And the problem at hand seems to be that—"

"Look, if we don't move more quickly," Kurt interrupts, "Cooper will lose his home by the time we assess the situation."

"Well, let's dive in then," Adam says, looking into the backseat, where Simon and Walter and Bryce are squished together, various electronic devices on their laps. "Simon, you did research before coming down here. Tell us everything you know about dairy farming."

Pleased to be called upon first, Simon clears his throat and announces that the history of dairy farming in the country is not an uplifting story. "Most small farmers have been driven out of business, thanks to a set of antiquated rules and regulations." He shuts his eyes and launches into a lengthy explanation of how a Byzantine milk-pricing system developed by the federal government in the 1930s, coupled with a thirty-year freeze on the wholesale price of milk, have made it impossible for most family farms to stay in business.

"How have any farms kept afloat if that's the case?" Jesse asks.

"The usual stuff," Simon answers. "Government subsidies, growth, economies of scale."

Jesse's not sure what any of that means.

Adam jots down a note: *Would expanding operations increase profit margins?*

"Despite our country's impressive population growth," Simon continues, in full lecture mode, "there are fewer farmers now than there were at the time of the Civil War. In fact, it's accurate to say that they've become a statistically insignificant number."

Kurt rolls his eyes. "I don't see how this relates to the crisis at hand."

"Well, it could be helpful to know if Cooper's milking the same number of cows as his father and grandfather did, for instance," Adam says.

Kurt passes a small truck. "I'm all for due diligence," he says tersely, "but Tuckington Farm is under *siege* here and we need to take action. We're leaving on Saturday, and there's no way we're going to become experts on the dairy-farming industry by then. What we need to do is get Cooper to explain what led to the foreclosure notices and how much time the bank is giving him. Next, we need to see his books and figure out a plan."

"But Cooper hasn't even let us know that there's a problem," Adam says. "How do you propose we get him to open up?"

"We just tell him we know he's fucked and that we're ready to help. Hell, as you said, there's some pretty impressive brainpower in this truck." Kurt glances at his reflection in the rearview mirror. "Just because some small-town bank lobbed a bomb his way doesn't mean we can't send up a few missiles of our own."

"My feeling is that we have to approach Cooper with care," Adam cautions. "If he wanted our help he'd have asked for it."

"The man's whole world is about to implode. What he needs is straight talk, not kid gloves," Kurt insists, gripping the wheel tightly. "And we can't help him without the facts."

Jesse, sitting in between Kurt and Adam, can't take the tension and starts rummaging through the glove box, where, amid the usual debris of maps, receipts, and registrations, he finds a cowbell and a photo of a young Cooper holding his father's hand.

Adam takes the photo from Jesse and studies it closely. Cooper is about seven and he and his father are standing in front of the Cow Palace, both looking incredibly proud. The inscription on the back reads: *Cooper's first milking, 1972.*

"I have an idea," Bryce says from the backseat. "To get our creative juices flowing, let's brainstorm!"

Kurt slaps a palm to his forehead.

"We do this in advertising all the time," Bryce tells the men. "Just free-associate. Be open and nonjudgmental."

"This isn't a game," Kurt yells.

"Come on," Bryce says. "Anyone? Just toss out the first crazy idea that pops into your head."

"How about Walter gets NBC to do a special on Tuckington Farm?" Simon suggests.

"Right," Kurt guffaws. "The headline: 'Tuckington Farm Exists.' *60 Minutes* will be pissed they didn't break the story."

"Ignore him," Bryce says.

"What about creating an adjunct business, like a bed-and-breakfast or dude ranch?" Jesse suggests.

"Great!" Simon says. "And I'm sure we could tie it to any number of historically significant Civil War battles fought in the vicinity. That might even dissuade developers from trying to build."

"Or Lucy could find an endangered bird," Jesse says.

"Loosen up a bit more," Bryce says. "Think outside the box."

Walter pokes at his Blackberry. "How about harvesting bull semen and selling it over the Internet? Is Pinckney a pedigree?"

"This is ridiculous," Kurt says. "Haven't any of you *ever* run a business? A lemonade stand even? The rule for profit is simple: raise production, lower costs."

"That's not all there is to it," Bryce says. "Production is only half the game; selling is the other half. In advertising, you have to find what we call the 'unique selling proposition' of a product."

"It's *milk,* Bryce," Kurt says. "There's nothing unique about it."

"That's where you're wrong," Bryce says. "Think Starbucks. Why do we pay four bucks for something we could buy elsewhere for one? Or two bucks for bottled water when tap water is free? It's about quality and branding and targeting your market." He draws a quick sketch of an old-fashioned milk bottle with a smiling cow on the label. "Tell me city folks won't pay out the wazoo for milk in fancy glass bottles," he says, presenting his illustration to them. "Slap on a label that says, 'Fresh from Tuckington Farm,' and *cha-ching.*"

Jesse tries to estimate how much he spends on organic produce at Whole Foods, a store so expensive that his sister calls it Whole Paycheck. "Bryce has a point."

"Gentlemen," Adam says, trying to diffuse the tension, "I don't think these approaches are mutually exclusive."

"Come on, Kurt," Bryce says. "Throw out an idea."

"I'm afraid I can only think inside the box on this one," he says. "I'd like to get some accurate numbers from Cooper, spend a little time with my calculator, and get my banker to secure some kind of short-term, low-interest loan or sale-and-lease-back plan that would give Cooper an infusion of cash up front and get him back on his feet."

Kurt's realism silences the men.

"Then we figure out what needs to be done differently around here," he adds.

Adam stares out the window. The sun is making its afternoon journey and its light slants across the hills, giving them a yellow glow. He lets his eyes relax and his mind wander, and tries to connect the dots and develop a behavioral-economy model that would explain Tuckington Farm's failure.

Kurt takes the Clover Hollow exit off the state road and

says, "Where to now?"

Jesse studies the directions. "I'm not sure," he says, getting fidgety again. "Cooper's directions don't make any sense. 'Exit at Clover Hollow and drive five miles past where the *old* Same station *used* to be. Then hang a left onto Lee Street, just beyond the frame house that once *was* the Hitching Post. From there, take a right into the *old* Farber's Pharmacy and park in the lot behind it."

Adam makes another note: *Could the crisis at the farm relate to Cooper's being stuck in the past?*

In Clover Hollow, they get directions to the pistol range and soon are where they're supposed to be, parked beside Cooper's truck in front of a nondescript, beige warehouse. They enter the range through a long corridor bordered by glass cases filled with pistols and ammunition, at the end of which is Cooper, engaged in an animated conversation with the burly old man behind the register. On the counter in front of him are a half dozen guns, headphones, goggles, and a stack of human-silhouette targets.

Cooper sees the men and waves them over. "You guys are going to love pistol practice. There are few things that relieve stress more than shooting up one of these," he says cheerily, holding up the target, a poster of a blue block person, round head atop rectangular body, five concentric ovals dissecting its torso. "These demarcate the kill zone," he tells them, using his gun as a pointer. "Hit anywhere in here and you do some major damage to vital organs, chances are, killing your victim." He gestures to the areas outside the circles. "Hit out here and you only wound your man; he can still shoot you back."

Adam wonders how Cooper can be so cavalier, given the gravity of the situation at the farm, and concludes that this, too, must be part of the problem.

The campers don their goggles and headphones, and follow Cooper into the range, where they pass alleys with older couples, men with their girlfriends, even whole families.

"Just another wholesome afternoon of teaching little Bobby how to kill," Bryce jokes.

The majority of the lanes, however, are filled with lone men shooting rapid-fire at targets sporting real images: Osama bin Laden, Hillary Clinton, Dr. Phil. Three men shoot .44 Magnums, guns so powerful that the campers' headphones compress against their ears when rounds are fired.

"Serial killer, serial killer, serial killer," Adam whispers as he passes these guys.

The gear is slightly disorienting, especially the headphones, which amplify voices one moment and turn off entirely the next to protect them from sudden loud sounds; it's the audio equivalent of a strobe light. The guns feel heavy and cold in their hands.

Settling into the alley farthest from the entrance, Cooper clips one of the blue silhouette sheets onto a pulley system and flips a switch that sends the target down the alley. "You hold the gun like so," he says, clutching it in his right hand with his arm extended almost straight. "And you lock your left hand around your right. Then relax, release the safety, square your target in the sight, and squeeze the trigger." Cooper squeezes and squeezes and squeezes, firing every round in his magazine with brass shell casings ejecting every which way, ricocheting off the walls. Finally, he stops, lowers his gun, and flips the switch, bringing the target forward. Fifteen holes are tightly clustered in the two centermost rings.

Kurt lets out a whistle. "Damn, that's some shooting."

Cooper grins. "Not too bad, if I do say so myself. I'm going to unload another magazine and then set you guys up in your own alleys."

The campers nod, but only politely, and when Cooper turns his back to shoot again, they look at Adam to initiate the conversation.

Adam doesn't feel so sure about confronting a man with a gun. "Um, Cooper," he says cautiously. "The guys and I would like to talk to you about something."

"Yep," says Cooper, raising his gun and squeezing off the first round.

Adam works up his courage. "We know about the foreclosure situation. We saw the notice and the sheriff's deputy leaving the scene." He pauses, waiting for a reaction, but Cooper just keeps shooting.

"The good news is we've come up with some really great ideas on how to help," Bryce says enthusiastically.

Cooper's aim suddenly loosens, and bullet holes spread out along the target. "Great ideas, huh?" His gaze is still fixed on the silhouette. "Thanks, that's very kind of you boys, but I have the situation well under control. Now, how about you get in your alleys and give this a go?"

"We actually had something else in mind," Kurt says forcefully. "We thought we should all spend the rest of the afternoon in your office and get to the bottom of this before you lose your farm."

Cooper lowers his gun and faces the campers. His eyes are narrow slits of concentrated disdain. "And what exactly would be the point of that? Y'all don't know shit about cows or farming."

Simon, Bryce, and Jesse take several small steps backward and Cooper realizes he's scared them. "Look, gentlemen, I don't mean to come across as unappreciative, but this is a private matter and one you know nothing about. The fact is, things *have* been rough, but I've straightened it all out today. End of story."

"Mind telling us how?" Kurt asks.

"If you must know, the bank has agreed to give me a little more time, and I plan to have an auction after you leave. I'll sell off some livestock and equipment, get the cash I need to pay off the farm's debts, and then start up operations again."

Kurt looks skeptical.

"This is how farmers do it," Cooper says.

"It's how farmers fail," Kurt says, taking out his calculator. He shakes his head when he realizes he has no numbers to plug in. "Look, I have no idea how much you can get for your cows and machinery in auction," he says, "but common sense tells me it can't be enough to pay back your debt *and* buy new livestock and equipment. Have you even considered the capital gains taxes you'll have to pay? None of this adds up. You'll be left with nothing to start up operations again."

Then Jesse inches forward. He speaks to Cooper the way he talks to authors who don't want criticism. "What I think Kurt is trying to say is that you have nothing to lose by letting us help," he says. "If we team up, I bet we can solve the problem once and for all."

This silences Cooper.

"I know we might seem like nothing more than a bunch of sissy city boys to you," Adam says, "but we actually *know* stuff. I'm getting my PhD in economics. Walt's a producer. Kurt runs his own software company."

"I've taken three businesses out of bankruptcy," Kurt adds.

"Just let us have a look at the numbers with you," Adam says.

The alley is ringing with guns exploding, targets zipping back and forth, men unleashing their pent-up frustrations, and suddenly Cooper feels tired, very tired. He stares for a long while at the target he's filled full of holes. "I suppose it can't hurt to take a little look-see," he says, and very slowly his taut facial muscles relax into unmistakable relief.

MARTHA AND LUCY are back in the kitchen once again, preparing for the party: arranging flowers, washing vegetables, wrapping silverware in napkins. Beatrice has just ordered fifty pounds of ribs and gotten in touch with the last of her neighbors to coordinate who's bringing what when she suggests a walk. "How about I show you girls the venue?" she says. "It's less than a mile from here."

The girls have been waiting for this moment all day and can't get out of the kitchen fast enough. They dry their hands, grab their jackets, and call to Tor and Tap, who bound over, delighted at the prospect of a walk. They set out on the gravel drive, cross the cattle grate, and make their way along the dirt road. The sky is marvelously clear and as they walk, they can hear distant sounds: children playing on a neighboring farm, cowbells on the other side of the knoll, a truck laboring up a nearby hill.

"You gals are going to love the old green barn. It's a very special place," Beatrice tells them. "You'll understand when you see it."

"Why isn't it used anymore?" Martha asks.

"We still use it," Beatrice says. "We pen the calves there and store hay in the winter. Nothing on this farm ever goes to waste. It's just not the main barn anymore."

"Why are the calves separated from the rest of the herd?" Martha asks.

"Because we're a *dairy*," Beatrice says slowly, regarding Martha with bland bovine patience. "Would you have us feed our profits to the calves?"

Martha's cheeks flush, but she still doesn't get it.

"What exactly do you think calves eat?" Beatrice asks.

Lucy pantomimes milking and, humiliated, Martha finally understands.

They pass deceased tractors and broken-down mowers with blades that look old enough to be museum artifacts, and Martha fantasizes that someday Beatrice, too, will be a rusted relic of Tuckington's past.

They're almost to the top of the hill when Beatrice mentions that Jolene will be joining them. "She'll be such a help. She's a real whiz at parties."

Martha searches her pockets for her cigarettes, which she finds in her jacket.

"To me, Jolene epitomizes what a woman should be," Beatrice says. "She's brilliant and talented, and yet still has enough charm to make any man feel smarter and taller and better-looking than he actually is."

"That's quite a skill," remarks Martha, imagining a sea of Lilliputian men around her ankles. "What does Jolene do for a living?" Martha imagines she's a cupcake froster.

"She's a livestock veterinarian."

When they get to the top of the hill, they see the old timber-frame barn nestled into the slope below them. It's so perfectly dilapidated and picturesque that it seems more like a romantic notion of a barn than an actual place where cows live. The barn is rustic and simple, with a slightly bowed roof and huge wagon doors opened wide and welcoming. They enter and walk down a central aisle on either side of which are stalls where calves are kept; above them is the huge hayloft where the party will take place. Their arrival disturbs swifts and starlings, which swoop out through the enormous side windows used to pitch hay through to wagons below. From inside, the barn looks like a great upturned boat, with rafters from front to back, thirty-foot-high ceilings. It smells like the very passage of time.

"Could there be a more perfect place for a party?" Martha asks.

For once, Beatrice agrees with her.

The afternoon is mild and a sweet-smelling breeze rustles hay on the floor. "How about we have the band at the far end, and the bar and food right here by the stairs," Martha suggests, gesturing with her arms. She closes her eyes and pictures how the barn will look from the outside when it's full of people dancing, and how the light and noise will contrast with the dark and quiet of the rest of the farm.

"I'm afraid that would never do," a voice from behind them says.

Lucy and Martha turn around. The voice belongs to a ripe young woman with an abundance of wavy chestnut brown hair and adorable dimples. She's sitting on a square bale of hay to one side of the stairs, and Lucy and Martha realize they must have walked right past her.

"Jolene, honey," Beatrice says, walking toward her with outstretched arms. "Have you been waiting long?"

"Just a few minutes," Jolene says, springing up to greet Beatrice, after which she saunters toward Lucy and Martha. "I hope you don't mind me adding my two cents. I just think it would be a mistake to create a logjam at the entrance. You'd be smarter to put the food closer to the band, to keep things circulating." She shakes Lucy's hand first, then turns to Martha. "So you're Martha."

Her voice is like a lullaby, musical and calming at once. Jolene is extremely pretty, with the type of smooth skin, blue eyes, and shiny hair that can only be described as wholesome. "The problem with putting it where you suggest is that it will cut into the dance floor," Martha says. She points to a spot halfway in between. "What about there?"

"Um. Not a good idea," Jolene says.

"Definitely not," Beatrice agrees.

Jolene shows Martha two massive cutouts in the floor. "No reason a city girl would know about them," she says. "They're for lowering hay." Her laugh tinkles. "They certainly make for a hazardous dance floor!"

Martha sees their point.

"Thank God you're here, honey," Beatrice says to Jolene. "We'd have men falling through the cracks without you!"

Martha joins Lucy, who's standing off at a distance, staring out one of the side windows.

Beatrice and Jolene don't seem to notice their absence and continue to make decisions as if they share one big party-planning brain: "Tables here?" "Absolutely." "Flowers at the top of the stairs?" "Perfect."

"Don't we get any say in this party?" Martha asks.

"Not by standing over here," Lucy says. "Get back in there and stand up to them."

Martha takes a deep breath. *Be assertive. You're Sharon Stone in* Basic Instinct, she tells herself, *but with underwear.* She knows it's the wrong casting decision and lights up a cigarette for courage. With her first inhale, she feels some relief; with her second, the tension is blowing right out of her body. *It's just a party,* she reminds herself. Then she hears a shriek.

"Are you completely out of your mind?" Beatrice screams. "Who smokes in a barn? You want to burn this place to the ground?"

Martha looks stricken. Her eyes start to water and as she races downstairs and out of the barn, she overhears Beatrice cackle and say something about needing to start a Woman Camp.

Lucy chases after Martha, catching up just outside the barn. "What a complete bitch," she says, though even she can't believe that Martha lit up in the barn. They sit down on the hillside. "You okay?"

Martha shakes her head no. "You know the worst thing about the South? Southern women."

As if on cue, Jolene and Beatrice exit the barn.

"Now, Martha, I'm sorry if I startled you," Beatrice says. "It just took me by surprise that anyone could do anything so . . . so . . ."

Martha rises and toes her cigarette out in the dirt in front of her. "May I have a word with you in private?" She leads Beatrice around to the other side of the barn. "I'd like to know why you veto every idea I come up with."

"Don't be ridiculous," Beatrice says.

"I don't think I am. What is it you don't like about me?"

"Dear, I don't know you well enough not to like you. Now, I'm sorry if you don't like that I'm particular about not burning down barns, but that's just the way I am."

Martha shuts her eyes. The conversation is going nowhere.

"And frankly," Beatrice adds, lifting her chin defiantly, "I'm not used to being addressed this way and I don't like it." She turns abruptly and walks away from Martha, back around the barn. She starts up the hill and toward the road that leads back to the farmhouse.

"Stay," Martha whispers to Tor and Tap in an attempt to enlist them on her side, but they dash after their mistress.

"What on earth did you say to Beatrice?" Jolene asks Martha.

"Sadly, not half of what I wanted to."

"She's seventy years old!" Jolene says, talking to Martha as if she were a child. "There's no need to be disrespectful." She jogs ahead to catch up to Beatrice.

"Please tell me that woman isn't staying for dinner," Martha says to Lucy. "The idea of watching her flirt with Cooper . . ."

"Don't worry about Jolene," Lucy says, as they begin reluctantly following them back to the house, a few paces behind. "She's no threat. Cooper likes you."

"No threat," Martha says, watching Jolene's perfectly shaped bottom sway above her long, coltish legs. "No threat. No threat."

When the four women are almost to the driveway, Cooper's truck comes barreling around the bend in the opposite direction. Adam's beside Cooper in the passenger seat and the rest of the campers follow in the second truck.

"I wonder why they're back so early," Martha says.

Cooper slows down to say a quick hello, smiling politely at Jolene but saving his conversation for Martha. "I hope you understand if we're a little late for supper," he says. "The boys and I have a few things to take care of."

When Adam waves to Lucy, Jolene assumes she's the object of his greeting and gives him an enthusiastic wave back.

Lucy feels the hairs on her arm lift. "Did you see that?" she whispers to Martha.

"She's no threat," Martha says, imitating Lucy. "No threat!"

COOPER'S OFFICE IS CRAMPED and filthy, with yellowed milking charts tacked to the walls and a decade's worth of *National Dairyman* clippings scattered on the shelves. The men awkwardly arrange themselves on the banged-up furniture: a steel desk, a dented file cabinet, and three stools. Cooper, Adam, and Kurt stand, leaning against the walls.

"Where do we begin?" asks Cooper, suddenly overwhelmed.

"Why don't you start by telling us where you think things went wrong," suggests Jesse.

With that, Cooper begins to unload. He tells them that since he took over the farm at the time of his father's death, profits have slowly and steadily fallen. He doesn't understand why; he's doing everything exactly the same as his father did: same number of cows, same acreage used for crops, same blend of feed, same trucking company, same processing plant, same type of cows, same breeding schedule, same everything.

"That might be your problem right there," Adam says. "It sounds like you're farming imitatively rather than creatively."

"It's the only way I know," Cooper says.

"It's not always a bad thing," says Kurt, "but chances are, you're missing some opportunities."

From there, with Cooper's okay, the men agree to launch into an intensive fact-finding mission and question every standard operating procedure in effect at Tuckington Farm. They work all evening and through much of the night, and do the same the next day. Cooper has his regular farmhands resume their duties so that the campers can spend all their time studying milking charts, checking out competing processing plants and dairy co-ops, going online to research feed.

The men calculate the advantage of different land uses, consider cash crops, explore other breeds, and examine each phase of production. They find that over the past five years, Tuckington Farm's milk production has dropped from an average of sixty-four pounds of milk per cow per day to sixty, with Simon reporting that the region's average is sixty-eight. They learn that milk prices are highest in the fall and winter, coinciding with school lunches, indicating that Cooper should reverse his breeding schedule. Simon is especially pleased to have discovered the U.S. Geological Survey site, which color-codes land-use maps from satellites, providing detailed information on the chemical composition of soil to help determine where to plant which crops. They locate a dairy co-op that pays significantly more for raw milk than the dairy processor that Cooper's family has worked with for generations.

"There's one more thing I'd like you to consider," Kurt says. "Agricultural software."

"Sounds expensive," Cooper says.

"It'll be worth it," explains Kurt, who called his company earlier and put a team of employees on the project. "The latest dairy software programs can streamline your operations in ways you can't imagine. Picture each cow at Tuckington Farm having a transponder that keeps tabs on how much food she eats, how much milk she produces, the butterfat content of the milk, and so on. It'll enable you to track breeding history, semen inventory, the whole shebang."

Cooper still looks overwhelmed, but grateful.

"And if it's all the same to you," Kurt says, "I'd like to stick around for a couple of weeks and help you set up the system." Before Cooper has a chance to object, Kurt says, "I've already cleared my work schedule and it would be my pleasure."

CHAPTER 12

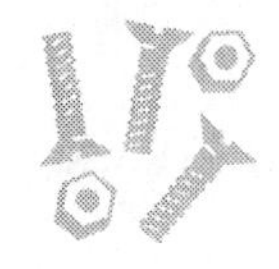

"Men marry women hoping they won't change. Women marry men hoping they will."

Anonymous

IT IS PAST MIDNIGHT when Martha sneaks down to the liquor cabinet, pours herself a rocks glass full of whiskey, and tiptoes back upstairs to her room. She brushes her hair and belts back enough of the drink to feel fortified, then opens the bedroom door and eases down the hallway, sliding along in stocking feet, a full moon illuminating her way. She passes the campers' bedrooms, the sofa where she and Cooper kissed, the hall bathroom with its dripping faucet, and stops in front of her destination: Cooper's bedroom.

There she hesitates and has to remind herself that she's going home in two days and needs to know where things stand. She empties the glass of whiskey, leaving the tumbler on the windowsill, and, without giving herself time to reconsider, grabs hold of the doorknob and slips silently into Cooper's dark room, pulling the door shut behind her.

For several seconds, Martha stands perfectly still, allowing her eyes to adjust to the darkness. Then, with one hand on the wall and the other waving back and forth in front of her to fend off furniture, she feels her way toward Cooper's bed, progressing only a short distance when the top of her head bangs into something large and hard, jutting out above her. Startled, her first thought (albeit irrational) is that Beatrice has set a trap for her. She reaches up and runs her fingers through what feels like the coarse, dry hair of a man's beard.

In her pocket she finds a book of matches and strikes one to discover that what she's bumped into is the hardened muzzle of some oversize member of the deer family: a moose? an elk? She's not sure which. Out of her peripheral vision, she sees that the entire wall is covered in hunting trophies—heads, antlers, an occasional whole animal—all casting gothic shadows of fairy-tale monsters, their lifeless glass eyes fixed on her.

It's not until the match goes out on its fall to the floor that Martha realizes she has dropped it. Suddenly, she can't reach Cooper fast enough and shuffles quickly toward him until her shins meet the side of his bed. There, her hands find space for her body to fit around his, and she climbs in, snuggling against his broad back. A subtle shift in his breathing indicates he's awake.

"Just in case you're used to buxom dairy maids climbing into bed with you," she whispers, "it's *Martha*."

Cooper exhales relief and laughs. "I thought I was in the middle of some fantastic dream and all I could think was, 'Don't wake up!' " He turns over to face her. "Hello, Martha."

"What's with the Museum of Natural History overhead?"

"Got you into my bed lickety-split, now, didn't it?"

"Hm."

Cooper wraps his arms around her. "I'm happy you're here. I've been hoping something like this would happen."

"Why haven't you done anything about it, then?"

"That's a good question," he says, caught off guard. "I guess I was taught that a proper Southern gentleman shouldn't crawl into his guest's bed."

"I suppose I have your mother to thank for that," Martha says. *Fucking Beatrice.* "You know, this Southern gentleman thing is starting to get on my nerves."

"A gentleman is really just a patient wolf."

"It happens to be a full moon tonight, wolfie."

Cooper howls softly.

"I imagine your mother wouldn't think much of a woman sneaking in here," Martha says. She listens for the sound of slippered feet in the hallway.

"Can't argue with you there," Cooper says. "Being direct is not part of her repertoire. To her, the art of being feminine is knowing how to make a man think that doing things *her* way was *his* idea."

Martha is impressed that Cooper understands this about his mother.

"There's a lot of craftiness with Southern women," he continues. "It's why I happen to be head over heels for a Yankee myself."

Martha smiles in the darkness.

"Remember what I told you at the Guggenheim? That I love how you always say exactly what's on your mind?"

"No," Martha lies.

"It's true. You are fearless!"

They kiss.

"Cooper?"

"Yes?"

Martha rolls onto her back. "If you had any idea how much whiskey it took to get me in here, you'd know I'm not fearless." Her eyes have finally adjusted to the darkness and she stares at a barely visible constellation of glow-in-the-dark planet stickers that must have been affixed to his ceiling when he was a child. She tries to summon up the little speech she prepared earlier in the day. "I think the only way to be fearless in love is to have total trust. I've spent the whole week making excuses for your behavior, but now I just want to know: Have you changed your mind about me?"

"Oh Martha, it's not that," Cooper says, pulling her closer still. He kisses the side of her forehead. "You *are* fearless and I'm a complete idiot."

They lie silently in the darkness for a long while; Martha focuses on the jutting chin of a black bear above her and Cooper struggles to find the right words.

"I'm not the kind of man who asks for help or talks things out," he finally says. "I wasn't brought up that way and it doesn't come naturally to me."

"Well, sneaking into your room in the middle of the night wasn't exactly natural for me, either," Martha says. "Now it's your turn to go out on a limb." She waits a beat. "I'll get you some whiskey if you want."

Cooper takes a deep breath. "I guess what you need to know is that I haven't been totally up front with you."

Martha stiffens, bracing herself for mention of Jolene.

"My farm's in trouble," he blurts out. "Very serious trouble."

Oh, that, Martha thinks. "I don't want to sound insensitive, but I don't understand why that should affect how you feel about me."

"Well, it doesn't effect how I *feel,* but at the risk of sounding sexist, I am a man. I can't very well pursue you if I can't provide for you, let alone myself."

There's something that no New York man would give a second thought to, Martha thinks. "So your solution is to dump me?"

"Of course not! Though, now that you put it that way, I can see how you might have misunderstood. The truth is it never occurred to me that I had the right to court you while my livelihood was falling apart. I was thinking of a postponement more than anything else . . . until I landed on my feet again."

"When were you going to let me in on this little romantic postponement? I think I had a right to know." Martha flips back on her side, so that their faces are just a few inches apart. "It's ironic, isn't it? I've brought all these men here to learn from you, and you stand to learn just as much from them." She puts a hand on his cheek. "I have news for you: I didn't fall for you because I thought you were a great dairy farmer."

"I know you didn't. But as crazy as it sounds, it matters to me that you do." Cooper considers all that he has learned from the campers in the past two days. "Look, Martha, it's becoming painfully clear to me that my way of doing things isn't working, but I'm trying to figure things out." He takes both her hands in his. "Will you please give me another chance?"

"I think that can be arranged," Martha says, smiling, "under certain conditions."

"Shoot," Cooper says. "Though I'm hoping it doesn't involve yoga or facials."

"Number one: call off your mother. Number two: don't shut me out again. And three"—here Martha pauses to work up her courage—"leave all that Southern gentleman crap at the bedroom door."

"Done, done, and most especially done!"

They stay awake until dawn, until the sun comes up over the hills, until Cooper, exhausted and happy, announces that he has cows to milk.

He gets dressed and sits on the edge of the bed, fingering one of Martha's dark curls, a long tendril that's splashed across the pillow, and tells her the whole story of how the campers came to his rescue. "I'm not exaggerating when I say that if it weren't for you and your nutty Man Camp idea, I might be well on my way to losing my family's farm."

Martha smiles.

"I happen to be falling in love with you, Martha McKenna," he says.

"Say that again," she whispers.

A few hours later, Martha sneaks out of Cooper's room and creeps back down the hall, scarcely able to believe she's gotten away with it. She gets dressed and skips downstairs, singing out, "Good morning," to Lucy and Beatrice, who are puttering in the kitchen.

"Good afternoon," Beatrice says pointedly.

Martha looks at the wall clock: twelve-twenty. "So it is! Sorry I overslept. Did I miss anything?"

"Not a thing," Lucy says, detecting the tremor of a secret in her friend's voice. She hands Martha a mug of coffee and mouths, *Did* I *miss anything?*

Before Martha can respond, Beatrice hands her the rocks glass she left on the windowsill outside Cooper's bedroom. It is freshly washed, warm in her hands. "Would you be a dear, Martha, and put this back where it belongs?"

THE CAMPERS SPEND the day hard at work trying to save Tuckington Farm. Walter reconfigures Cooper's computer with a wireless Internet connection and adds enough memory to accommodate the agricultural software program that Kurt's New York team has acquired and is modifying for the farm. Simon continues to pursue his soil research, color-coding a map of the farm, field by field, based on chemical composition. Bryce sketches logos and designs labels, and Adam tests algorithms to measure production. Kurt and Cooper spend the day in town, negotiating with local bankers to lift the lien on Tuckington Farm now that they've secured promissory letters from New York financiers, friends of Kurt's willing to invest.

Not far away, Lucy and Martha cart party supplies to the old barn and, under Beatrice's watchful eye, begin decorating for their bash. The girls are impatient for Beatrice to leave so they can talk about Martha's night with Cooper, but she doesn't. Instead, she lingers over the arrangement of the flowers, supervises the folding of napkins, and straightens the tablecloths Lucy and Martha have placed on the serving table and bar. In the end, however, the barn looks perfect: romantic and festive with wooden boxes of red geraniums on the windowsills, strings of white lights hanging from the rafters, and jugs overflowing with tall sunflowers scattered about.

Not until late in the afternoon, when Lucy and Martha have returned to the house to get dressed for the party, do they finally have a moment out of Beatrice's earshot. Martha is trying on her barn-dance outfit bought at Barney's two days before leaving New York City: a big swishy skirt and a narrow, white top that scoops low over her décolletage, while Lucy's ear is pressed against the door, listening for creaking floorboards. When finally she's satisfied that they're alone, Lucy flops down on the bed. "Out with it!" she demands, and Martha, in a twangy country accent, sings, *"I'm just a girl who can't say no!"* Swooshing her skirt back and forth, she dances around the room and divulges every detail of her night of lovemaking. Between talking about Cooper and putting on the ensemble, Martha is on top of the world. "I could be the lead in *Oklahoma.* Isn't this dress fun?"

"Yes, fun, very fun," Lucy says, more interested in Martha's romance with Cooper than her outfit. Not much of a shopper herself, Lucy's wearing a dress she's had for nearly a decade, a simple blue sheath that falls just above her knees and has a square neck bordered by tiny daisies. "Tell me how great it is to finally be with a man like Cooper."

"You know, nothing is ever as you think it's going to be," Martha says, making a face in the mirror as she puts on mascara. "Cooper doesn't have the weaknesses we're used to in men, but he doesn't have the strengths, either."

"What strengths?"

"Well, for one thing, our city boys know how to talk about feelings."

"Um. A week ago you would have called that whining, Martha."

"Well, try doing without it altogether and you have Cooper. Of course, he excels at being masculine and chivalrous, but he's not so hot when it comes to emotional stuff," she says, explaining how he was willing to risk their budding relationship rather than discuss his failures.

"Is it really too much to ask for both?" Lucy groans.

"Apparently so! Now, are you ready yet?" Martha asks, grabbing her friend's hand and pulling her off the bed.

Downstairs, they find Beatrice gazing out the kitchen window watching thunderheads roll in and settle over nearby hills. "Don't you just love a storm?" she asks. The skies seem to darken as she speaks, turning a fantastic purple-gray.

"I know I do," Martha says, imagining the tempest to come when Beatrice learns that she and Cooper are in love.

"Well, that one's headed due east," Lucy says. "See how the anvil top is facing us? It indicates the direction the storm will travel."

"My God, the things you know," Martha says, impressed, scouring her brain for a single useful weather fact.

An orange tabby pours down the fence in front of the house, giving Martha a pang of homesickness. She misses Hannibal, and for the first time, thinks about how far away New York is from West Virginia.

"Damn cat uses my garden as his personal litter box," says Beatrice, whistling for Tor and Tap to chase it off the property.

THE BAND IS WARMING UP when the women arrive, and the barn is already full of neighbors and friends drinking ice-cold longnecks, tapping their feet on the solid oak floor. Martha hasn't seen Cooper since dawn and when her eyes find him onstage, holding and caressing his upright bass as if it were a large woman, she wishes she were in his arms instead. His head bobs sweetly as he strokes out the rhythm with his eyes closed, concentrating to keep order alongside a feisty banjo plucking out a conversation with a mandolin, a fiddle, a guitar, and an instrument Martha's never seen before, a jaw harp. The musicians play bluegrass and hillbilly, ragtime and old-timey, their fingers strumming and their bodies working hard, big drops of cartoon sweat collecting on their foreheads.

An impromptu square dance begins with Beatrice calling out moves. To start with, the men line up on one side of the hay-loft and the women on the other, bowing and curtseying, keeping a measured distance. But as Beatrice's calls become faster and more complex—Do-si-do! Allemande! Circle home!—partners intertwine and the room turns into an elaborate kaleidoscope of shifting shapes and patterns, the heavy floors flexing under the weight of so many people dancing in rhythm.

Adam stands on the sidelines with Jesse. All dances remind him of junior high school when, shy and self-conscious, he and his friends would congregate under the bleachers and evaluate the girls in lieu of asking them to dance. The Neola women are pretty tonight, decked out in their party dresses, their lashes so thick with mascara that they look like dolls. Jolene, the prettiest of the bunch, emerges from the crowd, slightly tipsy from beer, and asks Adam to dance. She's the type of girl who wouldn't have noticed him in school but now, as thirty looms, she's casting her net a bit wider. He politely turns her down, explaining he promised his first dance to Lucy.

Adam scans the hayloft for Lucy and finds her on the far side of the square-dancers, laughing with Martha. The two are standing in front of the band, imitating Cooper's picking style on air basses, and Adam is struck by how stunning Lucy looks with her hair swept up off her slender neck. She is obviously taking great pleasure in Martha's happiness and there's an ease to her smile that hasn't been present for a long time, which makes Adam wonder if somehow he has been responsible for its absence. He recalls how disappointed she was on Valentine's Day.

What on earth am I waiting for? Adam suddenly wonders. He knows his dissertation will be finished soon and that countless jobs will come and go after that, but there is only one Lucy and she means everything to him. He decides on the spot to propose to her. Tonight. He tries to come up with some romantic way, but the crooning of a scraggly man at the mike—*"Why don't you love me like you used to do?"*—makes it impossible to concentrate, so he sneaks off to the empty silo attached to the barn where it's quiet. He paces in large circles to practice.

"Lucy," he says out loud, "I'm not particularly good at this kind of thing. . . ."

"Lucy, I think you know how I feel about you . . ."

"Lucy, we've been together for over two years now . . ."

"Marry me, Lucy," is what he finally decides upon. It echoes nicely in the silo and is strong, simple, and to the point.

"WOULD YOU LOOK at my baby brother go?" Martha says, watching Jesse promenade to the left with a pretty girl.

Lucy surveys the campers, who are busy flirting and fetching drinks. The local girls are all over them, hanging on to their shoulders, laughing at their jokes, leaning in to whisper secrets. "I can't believe these are really the same guys you had all those bad dates with."

"*You* can't believe it!" Martha says.

The band switches to a country-western song and the dancers pair off.

"Looks like we even have to give Beatrice some credit for the two-stepping lessons," Lucy says. "Look at them go."

Martha reluctantly agrees, watching Simon confidently turn a girl in a swirling skirt across the floor. "Man Camp has exceeded my every expectation."

"Adam's been acting like a different person," Lucy says. She cranes her neck around to look into the corners of the barn.

"Where is he, anyway? I haven't even had a dance yet."

When the band takes its first break, Cooper makes his way across the room toward Martha, but Beatrice intercepts him with a tall glass of lemonade.

"Thanks, Mom," he says, taking the glass but still focusing on Martha, who is now walking toward him.

"That was wonderful, honey," Beatrice says, moving in close. "I was wondering if I might have a word with you?"

Martha slows down slightly, unsure if she's welcome, but Cooper reaches for her hand over his mother's shoulder, and in a second she is standing by his side. "You look beautiful," he says, kissing Martha lightly on the mouth.

Beatrice adamantly tilts her head in the direction of where she wishes to be talking to him—alone—but Cooper shakes his head. "Whatever you have to say can be said in front of Martha," he tells her.

"Well, I was just hoping you'd ask Jolene to dance," Beatrice says. "I'm sure Martha wouldn't mind. I don't think it's polite to neglect old friends just because new friends are visiting."

"I've been playing my bass, Mom. I'm not neglecting anyone," Cooper says, and senses Martha scrutinizing his words. "In any case, I'm afraid my dance card's full tonight." He pretends to look at it: "Martha, Martha, Martha, Martha, Martha."

Martha smiles victory at Beatrice. *His dance card is full forever, baby.*

Beatrice tilts up her chin and walks back toward the bar as if the conversation never took place.

Soon after the band starts up again, Jolene sashays over to Martha. "Who's that?" she asks, directing her gaze at Kurt.

Martha admires her chutzpah, but can't tell if Jolene is interested in Kurt or just trying to appear uninterested in Cooper. "His name is Kurt. He's single, smart, and very successful . . . and staying at Tuckington Farm for an extra two weeks."

Jolene studies him.

"Here's a tip for you: he once told me he loves women with sad eyes," Martha says, trying to extend an olive branch. "I'd be happy to introduce you."

"No need," Jolene says, smoothing her skirt with the palms of her hands. She looks up, erases her pretty smile, and heads toward Kurt with an expression suggesting her puppy just died.

Martha laughs, unable to stop herself from admiring Jolene's ability to get into character.

—

On the band's next break, Martha corrals Lucy and Cooper into a Man Camp counselor conference, hustling them downstairs past the calf pens and outside, where the fragrant West Virginia evening rises up around them. The sky is churning, and she guides them along the wall of the barn on the hillside, where they're protected from the rain by an overhanging roof.

"A toast," Martha says, lifting her bottle. "To Man Camp!"

"To Man Camp," Lucy and Cooper toast back.

Martha takes a long pull on her beer, giddy with the week's success, especially her own with Cooper. "And to the finest counselors anywhere."

"Hear, hear," Cooper says.

"I'm still in shock we pulled it off," Lucy says.

"Well, we did," Cooper says. "Did you see how well the guys were doing in there? The ladies love them. And I'm happy to report that every camper passed basic automotive, carpentry, electricity, and firearms. With the exception, of course, of Bryce."

"Poor Bryce," Lucy says.

"He'll do fine," Martha assures them. "He's a creative guy with a good job and lots of style. That'll be enough for most women."

Cooper nods agreeably. "I'm ready to start planning next year's Man Camp whenever you are."

"Next year's?" Martha says. "How about next month's?"

"Hold your horses, both of you," Lucy says. "I still want to talk about this Man Camp. Who do you think got the most out of it?"

"As in who's the most improved camper?" Cooper asks.

"Yes."

"Easy," Martha says.

Adam returns from the silo to the hayloft, a man on a mission. "You seen Luce?" he asks Jesse.

"She was looking for you just a little while ago," Jesse says. "I think she walked outside with Martha."

"I better go find her," Adam says, wanting to act quickly while his courage is up. As soon as he gets outside, he grabs a handful of daisies growing alongside the wall, and follows the sound of Lucy's voice, loud and giddy with laughter, around the back side of the barn. He stops before making the final turn so that he can compose himself and rehearse his proposal one more time. The wind has picked up and rain is falling, and his future bride is just a few feet from him. He steels himself to interrupt their conversation when he overhears Cooper say, "Sure, Kurt came a long way, but the guy wasn't in terrible shape to start with."

"Think, Lucy," Martha says. "Who was in *really* bad shape from the very beginning?"

"They all were, weren't they?"

"You *honestly* don't know?" Cooper asks.

"Love is blind," Martha says. "Here's a clue: jumper cables."

Cooper whimpers a falsetto, "Something's out there in the woods and I'm *so* scared!"

Lucy's mouth drops open. "Adam is Most Improved Camper?"

"Hands down," Cooper says.

"Hear, hear," Martha says. "To Adam."

It's Cooper who sees Adam first, rounding the corner just as the three of them are toasting him, their beer bottles touching at shoulder height. If Adam didn't yet fully believe what he heard, there's no mistaking the panic that registers on their faces as he approaches.

"You brought me here *as a camper*?" he asks Lucy.

"Hey now, we're just messing around," Cooper says, stuttering slightly.

"You told them all about our Valentine's Day weekend?"

"It was all in good fun," Cooper says.

Adam gives him a sidelong glance and says, "What possibly gives you the right to criticize me? I helped save your macho ass." He looks back at Lucy, mortified that Cooper and Martha know all about his failings on their trip upstate. "You lied to me about coming here as a vacation?"

"Adam, let me explain—"

"You lied to me!" he repeats.

"Wait, Adam," Martha steps in. "Lucy didn't want to do any of this. I talked her into it."

"What difference does that make?" he asks, feeling terribly foolish. He drops the daisies on the ground.

"Oh Adam, please don't make this bigger than it is. You

caught us being silly and insensitive, and we are sorry," Lucy says. "*I* am sorry."

Adam turns on his heels to leave.

"Just hold up one second, Adam," Martha says. "I understand you're pissed off, and you have a right to be. But so does Lucy. We all know the woman's basically incapable of lying, so imagine what it must have taken for her to get you to come."

"So now I'm responsible for my girlfriend's deception? I don't think so." Adam looks disgusted and storms off.

Lucy starts after him and hesitates, uncertain of what to do.

"Just give him a little time," Cooper says. "He needs to cool off some."

"It'll be okay," Martha says.

"This is not going to be okay. Nothing about this is okay."

"Don't forget Adam's part in all this. Sending him to Man Camp wasn't a reward for good behavior. He's been a totally self-absorbed jerk and he's been ignoring your needs," Martha reminds her. "All you were trying to do was get things back on track. And as for Man Camp, it's been anything but a mistake. When has Adam *ever* stood up to you like that?" Martha puts an arm around Lucy, but Lucy shakes it off and runs after Adam.

When she gets around the barn, she sees she's too late. Adam's already in one of the trucks, speeding down the drive.

The taillights disappear over the hill and then reappear far in the distance across the pasture where the drive intersects with the street to town. Then they're gone.

CHAPTER 13

"What is most beautiful in virile men is something feminine; what is most beautiful in feminine women is something masculine."

Susan Sontag

ADAM'S EYES BLINK OPEN with Pavarotti's first shrill crow. Although the sun is barely up it seems impossibly bright and his head throbs from the base of his neck to his eyebrows. He concentrates on a blur outside the truck's window, focusing until he's able to make out the eave of the farmhouse. He must be in the driveway. The last thing he remembers is drinking whiskey at a local bar with a tough old guy who'd been a frogman in the Second World War.

What's he going to say to Lucy? At some point during the night, when his anger faded, Adam realized that what upset him most about the overheard conversation was the truth in it. Sometime in the last year he'd lost confidence and become terrified of Lucy's expectations. Adam covers his head with his arms and manages to fall back asleep, even though the rooster won't shut up.

Hours later, a tentative rap on the driver's-side window awakens him. He opens his eyes and sees Lucy standing outside with two mugs of coffee, struggling to open the door.

He pulls the handle and she climbs in.

"Hey," she says.

"Hey." He scoots over so that his back is against the passenger-side door and he can face her.

"I heard you drive in late last night but figured you needed some time alone or you would have come up." Her eyes are puffy and tired, and she looks unsure of what to say next. "You okay?"

"I've felt better," Adam admits, rubbing his head. He knows he must look like hell, probably smells even worse.

Lucy hands him one of the mugs of coffee. "Look, Adam, I feel terrible about what happened. I don't know what to say other than I'm very sorry I hurt you. There's no excuse for what I did."

"Don't," Adam shushes her.

They sit quietly and sip their coffee. The spring greenery is lush from the previous night's rain and a mourning dove flutters along the stone wall, piping out its lonesome song in a bid to impress a potential mate.

"Please say something," she says. "You forgive me, don't you?"

"Of course I do, Luce," he says. "I mean, do I wish you could have made your point some other way? Sure. But I understand that I didn't leave you with a lot of options."

Lucy exhales, shuts her eyes, and reaches for Adam's hand.

The dove catches the female's attention and bobs its head and fans its tail.

"I hope you can forgive me, too," he adds in a soft voice. "I know I've been a jerk. Somehow I got so absorbed in all that was going wrong with my life that I neglected the one thing that was going right."

Lucy squeezes his hand and Adam squeezes right back, and the two doves hop off the wall to continue their courtship out of sight.

Inside the farmhouse, the campers are gathered in the kitchen, where Beatrice holds court over one final breakfast feast: scrambled eggs, bacon and sausage, *and* pancakes.

"No one should ever have to decide between eggs and pancakes when it comes to breakfast," she says, nibbling on a crisp strip of bacon.

"We're going to miss your cooking, that's for sure," Bryce says, and the rest of the campers nod, one by one loading their plates and disappearing into the dining room.

Out of the corner of her eye, Martha spies a line of tiny ants marching up and over the kitchen island, alongside the platters of food. She frowns.

Noticing them at the same time, Bryce steps away from the counter with his breakfast.

Martha moistens a paper towel and prepares to obliterate the colony in a swipe, when Lucy walks in with Adam and says, "Stop. Don't even think about doing that!"

"Be serious, Lucy," Martha says. "They're *ants*!"

"Yes they are, and what you should be doing is studying them," Lucy says, motioning for Martha to come close. "Be careful where you step." Adam and Cooper lean in, too, and all four of their faces are lined up at counter level, inches from the ants. "Maybe give them a little of your pancake."

"There will be no feeding ants in my house, thank you very much," Beatrice says.

"You should try to *learn* something from them. Ants happen to be the world's most successful insect," Lucy tells them. "They've survived for over one hundred million years and there're probably a million *billion* of them on the planet at any time. They weigh more than all the birds, amphibians, reptiles, and mammals put together."

"That's just gross, Luce," Martha says. "Now, do you want to tell us what the big lesson is here, or are we supposed to wonder for the rest of our lives?"

"There's no big lesson." Lucy sighs. "More like something small to meditate on. Ants show us what can be accomplished with cooperation and hard work."

"That's our biologist," Cooper says.

Adam puts an arm around Lucy. "My biologist," he says.

While the girls are helping Beatrice clean the breakfast mess, Martha suddenly realizes how late it is. "All hands on deck," she shouts.

"Wrong metaphor," Lucy says. "Try something a little farmier."

"Let's git along, little dogies!" she calls up to the campers, who are in their rooms packing their bags.

"Better," says Cooper.

The campers make their way downstairs and stream through the kitchen and out to the truck. Lucy follows the pack, wanting to give Martha and Cooper some privacy before they are jammed into the truck along with the rest of the group for the two-hour drive back to the airport.

"When am I going to see you next?" Cooper asks, wrapping

his arms around Martha's waist. "Want to bring another group of men down or could I talk you into some one-on-one time?"

Martha smiles at the thought of Cooper all to herself. "There's nothing I'd love more than a little solo time with you."

A delicate cough alerts them to Beatrice's presence in the kitchen, and Martha quickly reconsiders. "What are the chances of you getting to New York any time soon?"

"So happens I might be coming up with Kurt in two weeks to meet with his investors. Can I stay with you?"

Martha blushes slightly, delighted by the question. "Of course you can."

Cooper gives her a squeeze and steps back. "Well, I guess it's about time I get this show on the road," he says, clapping his hands together and setting off to organize the campers.

Beatrice approaches Martha with outstretched arms. "It's been such a delight to have you here," she says, giving her guest a warm hug good-bye. "I hope it won't be too long before you visit us again."

"Thanks," Martha says awkwardly. She can't tell whether Beatrice is appeasing Cooper, trying to catch her off guard, or actually has had a change of heart. Could it be that she's just really happy to see me go? Martha wonders, making her way out onto the porch, where she joins Lucy, who is watching the campers.

"Do you think they're eager to get home or sad to leave?" Lucy asks.

"Probably a mix of both," Martha replies. "That's how it is for me, anyway. Part of me can't wait to be back in the city with all that's familiar: FirstDate, auditions, dial-up sushi, Hannibal. But the other part of me has really grown to appreciate what's timeless and reassuring about cows." She lights a cigarette and inhales thoughtfully. "And as you know, there's nothing like the love of a good man."

They watch the men toss their bags into the truck with ease. Walter kicks the tires; Simon takes in the scenery one last time; Jesse nuzzles Tap and Tor; Bryce swabs down the backseat with disinfectant wipes.

"I don't think your pal Bryce is going to miss a thing about farm life," Lucy says.

"Probably not, but I guarantee you the rest of them will. I think they got a lot out of coming here. Jesse, for instance, is about to take the first untranquilized flight of his life."

"Impressive."

"You and Adam doing okay?" Martha asks.

"We're good. We talked things out and not only did he own up to his shortcomings, he forgave me mine," Lucy says, glancing at Adam and Cooper, who are engaged in a private conversation. She hopes they are making amends. "When the gods want to punish you, they answer your prayers. I wanted Adam to be a stronger man. Now I have to learn how to deal with his strength."

Martha nods and takes another drag on her cigarette. "I wonder what Eva will have to say about all this."

Lucy laughs. "Do we have to tell her about getting lost in the caves?"

"Hell no! Only the good stuff."

When the truck is fully loaded, Lucy and Martha crowd into the front, where they sit in between Cooper and Adam. They wave good-bye to Beatrice and Kurt, who stand on the front porch with Tor and Tap on either side, looking like a country postcard. Then the truck lurches forward, rattles over the cattle grate, and rounds the bend, where they drive alongside a stretch of newly put-up fence, blond instead of gray. They pass the calf pasture, the Cow Palace, and a roadside ditch full of purple joe-pye weed. Lucy rests her head on Adam's shoulder and Martha watches Tuckington Farm recede into the distance, wondering about the possibility of living a life so unlike the one she's known. Cooper puts his arm around her and she knows that somehow she'll figure out a compromise.

They all will.

ABOUT THE AUTHOR

ADRIENNE BRODEUR is the founding editor of *Zoetrope: All-Story.* She lives in New York City.

ABOUT THE TYPE

This book was set in Baskerville, a typeface which was designed by John Baskerville, an amateur printer and typefounder, and cut for him by John Handy in 1750. The type became popular again when The Lanston Monotype Corporation of London revived the classic Roman face in 1923. The Mergenthaler Linotype Company in England and the United States cut a version of Baskerville in 1931, making it one of the most widely used typefaces today.

TEAR OUT PAGE AND FOLD ALONG DOTTED LINE

If you would like to share your thoughts on this book with us and your fellow booksellers, please do so here or send us an e-mail at RHTrademarketing@randomhouse.com

Title ______________________________

____

____

____

____

Name: ______________________________
Bookstore: ______________________________
Address: ______________________________

FOLD ALONG DOTTED LINE

PLACE
STAMP
HERE

RANDOM HOUSE
1745 Broadway, MD 18-2
New York, NY 10019
Attn: K. Ruden